a novel

DIDIER LECLAIR

Translated by Elaine Kennedy

MAWEN**Z**I
HOUSE

Originally published in the French language in Canada as
Toronto, je t'aime in 2000 by Les Édition du Vermillon

Published with the generous assistance of the Canada Council for the Arts and the Ontario Arts Council. We also acknowledge the support of the Government of Canada through the Canada Book Fund and the Government of Ontario through the Ontario Book Publishing Tax Credit.

We acknowledge the financial support of the Government of Canada.

Cover photo: "A Snowy Night, A Lonely Night" by Kurt Wang
Cover design by Sabrina Pignataro

Library and Archives Canada Cataloguing in Publication

Title: Toronto, I love you : a novel / Didier Leclair ; translated by Elaine Kennedy.
Other titles: Toronto, je t'aime. English
Names: Leclair, Didier, author. | Kennedy, Elaine, 1954- translator.
Description: Translation of: Toronto, je t'aime.
Identifiers: Canadiana (print) 20220195757 | Canadiana (ebook) 20220195838 | ISBN 9781774150665 (softcover) | ISBN 9781774150672 (EPUB) | ISBN 9781774150689 (PDF)
Classification: LCC PS8573.E3385 T6713 2022 | DDC C843/.6—dc23

Printed and bound in Canada by Coach House Printing

Mawenzi House Publishers Ltd.
39 Woburn Avenue (B)
Toronto, Ontario M5M 1K5
Canada

www.mawenzihouse.com

For Doctor Fulgence Kabagema — DL

For RJ — EK

CONTENTS

Cloclo,

My dear parrot, it's for you that I turn to the land of my birth in these pages. Of course there are people somewhere in the world who will read my story, but they don't have feathers like you or wings to fly up in the clouds. Readers are like me, whereas you have the distinction of being a bird that speaks, on top of being my childhood companion. There's nothing extraordinary about your grey plumage and clump of red tail feathers, I know. Yet given that whole part of the sky you cover when you fly and the thousands of exotic colours that have filled our lives, you deserve a novel addressed to you alone. I know you have your ear to the slightest sound and the tip of your beak on the pulse of the world. Just to take you on a different sensory track, I'm inviting you to fly my way, in the realm of the written word. The thrill isn't the same, but it's still there, with bursts of strong sensations, the bitterness of rare perfumes, and all the hues assumed by the tree-shaped sunlight rooted in the firmament.

First Impression

My first impression when I saw her was a sensation of height and density within a circumference. I wasn't struck by her eyes or legs, or even the way she moved. That was simply because she had many eyes, and a multitude of lives stirring within her. She fascinated me from the moment I caught sight of her. Her youthful appearance stemmed from her architecture, solidly anchored in the ground. She seemed to have shot up in a monumental and mind-boggling manner. There, from where I stood, an array of lines and curves stretched up and out before me. I scrutinized the cacophony of urban structures with the intensity and concern of a soul about to be swept off his feet. Naturally I didn't know her yet, and she terrified me a little. There's always something risky about love at first sight, but that was just another reason to fall for her. Not knowing anything about her, I imagined her the way I wanted her to be, imposing images on her that suited her beautifully—images from American films and magazines forever etched in my mind. With the sun reflecting on her, she seemed like a sort of sanctuary where my life would unfold. It's true that everything written or printed about her was generally in her favour. Postcards as well as television and radio advertising all cast her in a positive light. Yet it wasn't only her exotic aspect that won me over. Toronto enveloped me in her harsh grey factory fumes and surrounded me with the trees surviving in her very heart. This North American city knew how to captivate me with the hustle and bustle of millions struggling to refine their clamorous lives. She obsessed me so abruptly that she bewitched me before I knew what was happening. From the outset, Toronto showed me what she was made of, with her towers scraping the sky. She offered up her profile to me, which was a sort of wild gigantism amid a mosaic of colours.

The lawns of luxury houses springing up in the suburbs, the fruits displayed on sidewalk stands, the satiny blondness of the women, and so many other gems in this unfamiliar world captured my gaze, hungry for it all.

I know that, today, it might seem crazy to be in love with a city since they all copy one another and become unremarkable. Nonetheless, I can't deny it: I love Toronto. I'm aware that this doesn't make any sense compared to the love one might feel for another. Yet this is my fate, and I am a willing victim of it.

In July 1995, I finally arrived in Toronto, Canada. It wasn't a glorious day. It was somewhat gloomy, but setting foot in North America over-joyed me. With a vague smile and a light suitcase, I wandered through the corridors of Pearson Airport without really knowing where I was going. At first glance, the people were exactly as I'd expected: a crowd from a variety of backgrounds. Some were wearing suits and ties, others silk turbans, and still others, multicoloured Rasta caps. I'd seen this type of clothing in the many Canadian magazines I'd read in Cotonou, Benin.

Being one of the thousands of landed immigrants was a godsend for someone penniless like me. It meant that I'd be able to eat three meals a day for the rest of my life. It also meant that I wasn't going to become one of those wretched foreigners who's turned away by border officers everywhere and goes back home with shame in his eyes and nothing in his stomach. If there's one fear that haunts people travelling to a promised land, it's never being able to settle there. They can't return. Their native countries are never the same: it's as if their homelands knew these folks had tried to desert them. I've seen so many of these souls who wind up on the shores of prosperous nations, only to be turned back like debris swept out to sea. All those stranded have the same look in their eyes—that of a sail torn by a fickle wind averse to dreams. After being cast out, they lose their taste for life. They become impassioned only by discussions reminding them of the vision they held for their great adventure, now aborted. For a long time, I had a phobia about ending up with the same wooden look as those foolhardy people immigration officers reject by the dozen. Luckily for me, that was not the case.

I'd chosen Toronto because I wanted to see my old friend Eddy Kpatindé again. I'd written to him, telling him that I'd be coming. I hadn't heard from Eddy in two years and I wasn't sure that he still lived in the city. I decided to take my chances anyway. Unfortunately, I didn't see Eddy when I arrived at Pearson Airport. I dialed his number, and a strange man's voice confirmed that he still lived at the same address, but had gone to Montreal for a week. The man said that he knew I'd be coming and that he'd pick me up in about a half an hour.

On the Way to the City

I was sitting in a white Toyota moving at high speed toward an unknown destination. Completely stunned by the crazy traffic, I had great difficulty hiding my bewilderment from the two men who had met me at the airport. I had to bite my lip many times to stifle my gasps of wonder. The asphalt, the concrete, the glass—these elements of modernism so imposing in North American cities—commanded my respect given their volume and stability. After a while, the synchronized lights, roaring buses, and rush of raging engines dazed me somewhat.

The driver of the Toyota hadn't said a word. The man in the passenger seat, Joseph, hadn't stopped talking. It's hard for me to remember his long soliloquy since I wasn't paying attention. Groggy, I was gradually hypnotized by the driver's dreadlocks, which swung every time he so much as touched the brake. Joseph was quite tall, close-shaven, and his light brown eyes stood out against his matte black skin. He seemed easygoing and cheerful and looked like he was from the Bronx with his Malcolm X tee-shirt.

My gaze shifted from the lively, quick-moving scene outside to the cowry shells dotting the driver's hair. From the back, he resembled an illuminated satellite on its way to some strange universe.

As exhaustion descended upon me, I struggled to focus on my surroundings. Everything was becoming blurry, and Joseph's words no longer made much sense, just fusing into a Caribbean intonation and rhythm. This was the first time I'd felt drowsy since I left home, my excitement finally reaching the limit. I opened my eyes one last time upon brightly coloured billboards, then all I registered was a myriad of stars in the darkness of my sleep.

Arriving at Eddy's

I came back down to earth at the sight of Finch Avenue, dismal and seedy. The open space there revealed a sky as bare as the head of a crownless king. Studded with dreary grey high-rises, it gave me the impression of a gap-toothed jaw ready to close on me. The Toyota pulled into one of the huge parking lots by these buildings, where children were running this way and that, clutching shopping carts likely stolen from a local supermarket. After we parked amid the scramble of spirited kids, I lifted my head to look at the top of the tower in front of the car. The structure was a mile high. Surrounded by a few others close by, it made anyone who scanned the heights feel like Tom Thumb. Cramped balconies sat one beneath the other in a steep line down to the ground. The paint on the exterior of these apartments was peeling off in large patches, giving me an idea of the interior.

My arrival in this bleak locale didn't really break the spell of being in Toronto. Poverty and miserable dwellings had never surprised me. What shocked me though was that Eddy, a talented and ambitious artist, was living in such a dilapidated place. The mere idea that he hadn't yet made it big in the film world horrified me. Handsome, extroverted, and highly enterprising, Eddy had always struck me as the prototype of someone who would go far. It's true that I hadn't heard from him in a couple of years. To be honest, my fear that he was failing was simply a way of suppressing my own anxiety. I could already see myself rotting in the same type of hole. My dread of defeat grew as I walked toward the entrance with my escort. Just before disappearing into the dark front hall and being swallowed by the hideous building, I noticed shaggy heads at the edges of some of the balconies. Lifeless eyes peered down at me with the curiosity of the idle.

There were a lot more people milling about inside. The place was like an ant's nest with thin partitions, and the jumbled voices of residents could easily be heard. The narrow corridors were wallpa-pered in burgundy. The lighting was so murky that it was difficult to see the faces of those filing by.

The two men showed me into an apartment on the seventh floor, and Joseph led me to my room. I noticed that someone else's belong-ings were in it.

"Okay, here you are. Make yourself at home." That was all he said.

There was one bed. The room was so disorderly that it looked as if a hurricane had recently swept through. The walls were covered with an archipelago of posters, and their scattered placement, with no concern for right or wrong side up, added to the deranged atmosphere.

Seeing the stunned look on my face, Joseph explained, "Oh, this is Koffi's room. You can use the bed. He doesn't come home till really late or early in the morning. We'll see later on."

When the door closed, I sat down on the small bed. I wondered how Eddy knew these people. Maybe they were all artists. In any event, I was so tired that I had no intention of racking my brain. I lay down very slowly, the whistling of the airplane still in my ears. I felt drained from the long trip and empty inside. I had no idea what I was doing in this room. My mind was as muddled as the room was messy. A pervasive feeling of belonging to no one, of being in a no man's land, upset me enormously. I'd left Benin, but I wasn't convinced that I was completely in Canada. I'd lost touch with a part of myself along the way. That sense of insecurity created an abyss in my breast and sent shivers down my skin like flashes of lightning snatched from the night. I started to gasp, heavy grey clouds having formed in my chest. As I waited to feel whole again, tears rained gently down my cheeks, tracing erratic lines in search of a clearing.

Koffi's Heroes

When I woke up, I lay in bed for a few moments listening to the sounds coming through the window from the road below. I gazed at each of the posters in the room. Martin Luther King appeared on one of them, with that revindicating look that all black American preachers seemed to have inherited. Malcolm X was there as well, an accusing finger pointed at the photographer's lens. Bob Marley was up on the ceiling, a smile on his face and a guitar in his hand. To the left sat Toussaint Louverture on a horse. To the right was Lumumba in a suit and tie, Amilcar Cabral, and many others filling every square inch of the walls. Militant slogans were written under each of the images.

The breeze roused me more fully. I hadn't the slightest idea what time it was; day seemed reluctant to give way to night. I had to walk around the piles of newspapers on the floor to reach the window. Although it was open, I could smell the pungent odour of stale cigarette smoke, which kept making me clear my throat. When I glanced outside, I got quite a shock. I was at a startling height. Toronto was vast, extending for as far as the eye could see under squadrons of white clouds pierced by rays of sunlight. The people on the ground looked like elves continually on the move. I'd never seen such a dizzying spectacle of human life. Everything down there was pulsing with energy, and gigantic high-rises competed in reaching for the sky. The contrast between the old architecture of bell towers and the crushing modernism of new buildings suggested a waning of faith; the skyscrapers appeared to be the new confidants of the gods. That forest of concrete with sparkling windows, summits pointed like rebel spears, hazy roofs in the distance, and streets made narrow by the wonders of perspective—it all made my head spin.

I stretched out on the bed again and started reviewing my English as if cleaning a gun to ensure shooting accuracy. English is a language

I'd had to learn out of hunger. It's the language spoken in Cotonou
to buy and sell on the black market. In many cases, it's used to bring
in smuggled fuel, spare parts, and other products from neighbouring Nigeria. It's the language of the starving, but it's also the mother
tongue of an elderly white woman who works at the American cultural centre in Cotonou. Miss Colker would always come over to me,
with her soft hesitant steps, to tell me it was closing time. When I'd
see that lady, with her wrinkled face and sweet smile, walking toward
me, I'd get up without making her wait. I never learned much about
Miss Colker. All I knew was that she'd married a local man who had
died under questionable circumstances. In Africa, there are deaths like
that, deaths of which the cause remains unknown or unclear.

The bedroom door opened, and the Toyota driver told me with a
distrustful look that it was time to eat. In the living room, the television was displaying soundless pictures. Joseph was sniffing the food
in the saucepans on the stove. Singing to himself, he seemed satisfied
with the menu. Images of war were moving across the screen. Noticing
my interest in them, Joseph decided to share his opinion with me.

"Those people fighting . . . As far as I'm concerned, the Serbs and
Croats are one and the same!"

"I think so, too. So tell me, does Eddy live here?"

"Of course," said Joseph, still smelling the food. "Why? You think
someone's kidnapped him? Ha ha! Bob, Raymond thinks that some-
body's taken Eddy hostage."

Bob, the one with the dreadlocks, gave a mocking laugh.

"No I don't," I replied. "It's just that I didn't see anything that might
belong to him in the room."

"Oh you know Eddy. He's got a girlfriend who lives close to downtown. Most of his things are at her place. He took the rest of them with
him to Montreal."

I seized the opportunity to ask about Koffi.

"Well, he's quite a character!" said Joseph. "It's hard to describe Koffi
just like that. You'll see."

The First Supper

I knew that Bob and Joseph weren't directly from Africa the moment they spoke to me. But at the table, I couldn't help finding something familiar about their faces. In them, I recognized the tailor across the way from where I'd lived. I glimpsed a mean teacher I'd had as a child, the mouth of a neighbour, the nose of a cousin whose name I'd forgotten. I felt uncomfortable about it. This mixture of attraction and unease, of love and hatred, stemmed from an unconscious memory of slavery and its centuries of violence. We exchanged furtive glances that spoke of the bite of whips, the rattling of chains, and all the dealings from which many African peoples had profited.

Curls of steam rose from our plates, making the atmosphere opaque. The silence became heavy as Bob and Joseph sought the eye of a Judas, a traitor, a slave trader. I knew they were strangers, but something told me that I needed to be careful. Simply because with our history of blood, hatred, and humiliation, it was impossible for us to remain indifferent to one other. There would be friendship or loathing, brotherhood or rejection. I understood that I wasn't starting a relationship with them. I was continuing one that was centuries old. Nothing and no one could change that.

Koffi, Unlike Any Other

I wasn't able to fall asleep before the intriguing Koffi came home. Standing at the window, I practised getting used to the height of the apartment and looked out over the city, with its spectacle of lights. Everything was flashing—traffic lights, vehicle lights, shop signs. It was a magical dance for someone accustomed to candles like me.

I knew that Koffi was a West African name and I hoped that I didn't know this man. I didn't want to have travelled all this way to find myself sharing the room of an acquaintance, both of us nurturing the idea of forgetting our pasts and building new lives. As paradoxical as it seems, that could only be done with the help of an old friend, someone who inspires and encourages you in your attempt to turn the page and start over.

Koffi could well have been one of my creditors or the son of a previously rich man who looked down on the poor because of his past affluence. Or some shady character who had seen me going to Jonquet, the pleasure district in Cotonou. The posters of black heroes didn't prove anything about him. I'd often shouted "Long live the revolution!" while dreaming of getting the hell out of the country.

Around midnight, I heard the bedroom door open. An imposing figure appeared in the shadows. When the man finally switched on the light, I had trouble looking at him until my eyes adjusted.

"Are you Raymond? I'm Koffi," he said in a pleased voice. I didn't recognize his accent. He walked over to the closet while talking to me.

"Are you from the West Coast, like Eddy?"

"Yes, I'm from Benin."

"Benin!" he exclaimed in a reproachful tone, "that doesn't mean anything!"

"Why do you say that?" I asked, very surprised.

"The whites are the ones who divided up Africa. Benin doesn't mean anything. The borders are lies."

I thought I heard Joseph laughing in my ear, repeating that Koffi really was different. With his red hair, bulging torso and slim physique, he was no Adonis, but he had a set of muscles that would've impressed a good many people. After getting out a mattress, he quickly made up his bed on the floor and flicked off the light. He continued the conversation where he'd left off.

"Are you from Ouidah, like Eddy?"

"My mother's from there."

Koffi must have sat up, because I felt his gaze on me even through the darkness.

"And your father?"

"I never knew him."

Silence fell between us. My answers seemed to have made him stop and think.

"My name's John Boggel Grant, but everyone here calls me Koffi. One of my ancestors was captured by the Portuguese around 1830. He was a crab fisher from the village of Ouidah. His descendants kept his name, which was Koffi, as a family legacy."

I didn't know how to respond. I could hardly believe his story. It seemed so far-fetched. I didn't know what he expected me to say after making such a claim. Did he want me to tell him about my ancestors? I didn't know who they were. I couldn't even go as far back as my grandparents. What's more, I had no way of determining if he was telling the truth about Benin. I didn't know the history of the country well enough. I didn't know much about the whole tragic period of slavery either, so I decided to change the subject.

I asked him why he'd put up the posters every which way on the walls. He didn't reply, and lit a cigarette in the dark. He continued smoking for a good five minutes in silence. That was fine with me because I was very tired. I certainly didn't feel like talking about Benin. What was going through my mind that night wouldn't have made for very pleasant conversation. My thoughts had turned to an oppressive sun beating down on women peddlers bathed in sweat, unweaned children at their breasts. I could hear the deadly rains in poor districts. I could see lightning tear through gloomy skies and roads become riddled with water-filled holes. I didn't dare tell Koffi that I'd come to this new world to begin again and forget about the foodless days. I decided to keep quiet about my past, like a soul who's only just emerged from nothingness. Koffi ended up launching into a monologue on politics. He talked about Lumumba and building a better world for blacks around the globe. He held out his cigarette to me.

"Go ahead. I think you'll like it," he said.

Between his fingertips quivered a small evanescent glimmer. It was a friendly gesture. The first in this lightless room, in this city that bustles even at night. I took the joint right away, burning my fingers slightly. Picking up the reefer off the floor, I heard Koffi's throaty laughter, like a welcoming trumpet. I coughed on the first puff, which made him laugh even harder. Little by little, a warmth enveloped my body. My hair bristled, my hands trembled, my eyes bulged. Despite that, I felt completely aware of my thoughts and movements. Koffi's words seemed crystal clear, and I could almost guess what he was going to say. I focused on his melodious intonation, which transformed his speech into the music of wind chimes. Within moments, I felt light and ready to recover from my very long journey.

The Beautiful Maïmouna

I spent the first night dreaming about the most beautiful prostitute in Cotonou. Her name was Catherine Maïmouna Dossou, but she was known as the Bountiful Bijou. She had earned that name when her bosom could no longer suffer any bra.

Bijou and I were close neighbours. I'd always helped her mother out by ironing the laundry, repairing the motorcycle, or unclogging the septic tank. So, to Bijou, I was Raymond the handyman.

"Something's really bugging you," she said one evening when I was mulling things over down by the sea.

I didn't reply right away. I acted as if she hadn't spoken to me, so she'd understand that I wanted her to leave. Bijou was a prostitute for white men and she dreamt of marrying one. Not feeling able to compete with her clients, I stayed away from her. I refused to entertain the slightest notion that she could be mine, even for a few moments. She was forbidden on the basis of race, which made her even more attractive to me. A woman who sold her body to whites couldn't hang around with an unemployed guy who did odd jobs to survive. So I told her to go away.

"You're down here too much," she said. "Be careful you don't end up in the water!"

Seeing that I ignored her, she added, "You're an idiot! You can't even kill yourself. It takes guts to do that."

She fell silent for a moment, then began singing an old childhood song to herself. Something that reminded me of the Akpakpa district, its smells, its market, its merchants. One of those songs about a princess, a kingdom, and a wounded heart.

I continued to scan the skyline even though I was no longer immersed in thought. I peered into the distance to avoid Bijou's gaze, and I clung to an invisible vista to avoid falling into her arms and singing old fairy tales with her. Out on the water, a few waves rose up out of nowhere, their roaring muffled by the wind. Then gloom overcame the sky, totally indifferent to the world beyond the horizon.

Every evening, Bijou would prowl around the Sheraton Hotel like a feline on the lookout for prey. Her clientele included mainly public servants on a posting and professors teaching for a time in Africa. In other words, people trying to advance their careers by gaining experience on the continent.

Watching the ocean for so long, I lost track of time. The world was becoming one large ship for me, with only one way out—the water. I hadn't returned home in two days because my creditors were looking for me. I was waiting to come up with an idea, but deep down, I hoped that the universe would collapse.

Bijou's singing managed to disarm something in me. Without my realizing it at the time, she averted the horrific attempt I'd wanted to make on my life. Her little orphic song relieved me of the feeling that I was simply a bit player in a world where happiness remained distant and wealth inaccessible to the whore and the despairing poor.

At least Bijou, I thought, knew who she was bowing down to— white men. That wasn't true of a desperate guy crippled with debt. He could bow down to anyone. I felt warm tears roll furtively down my cheeks. Bijou stopped singing and wrapped me in her arms. Only she could understand the stars in my eyes. Only her soul could feel the weight of mine, dreaming of what was impossible to attain. That night, she could clearly see the flickering of my pain, and she dreaded the day I would commit the fatal act. I was finding it more and more difficult to go on without a plan. I knew full well that if I continued merely scraping by, I couldn't hope for a miracle. Poverty in the Third World wasn't merciful to anyone. You had to pray or resign yourself. I couldn't manage to do either.

Bijou brought her face up to my ear and her lips to my lobe, cooled by the wind. We lay down gently between two coconut trees right there in front of the sea.

How the Bountiful Bijou Managed to Console Me

Sitting up on the sand, she opened her legs slowly, undid my pants, and drew out my sex, which was half-convinced of what was going to happen. With a skilful hand, she ran her fingers along my member, caressing the pulsing veins swelling my desire. I shivered all the more in the cool night air as Bijou pressed her fleshy lips to my chest, which she had bared in no time. Then she lifted her thigh-high-slit evening dress and slid lasciviously onto my full erection, impaling herself. She began plunging fiercely as if to probe her innermost depths, and I felt her sex anointing my own as her yearning surged and her hair danced under the coconut trees. Dishevelled by the fitful thrusting of her feverish pelvis, she seemed to be wrestling with a different wind, to be driven by lustful gusts. Bijou was bouncing up and down on me, her cotton dress hugging her body. I clutched her ballistic breasts, which I squeezed every time we skimmed the crest. Bijou was literally jumping on me, making us groan. And all our high-pitched moans consoled me that sorrowful night. I slipped my hands along her gyrating hips, freeing her breasts in their frenetic trance. The thrill of being within her was finally too much for me. Hot and wet, I peaked with a furious, abundant, milky explosion within Bijou's inner night. She looked at me, dazed by the force of my torrent, her dress covered with foam, a tender smile appearing on her lips.

I often wondered why Bijou had decided to give herself to me. I had nothing to give her, the young woman who hoped to convince a white man to take her far away from her woes. Then, when I thought about it more, I understood. She'd recognized the distress in my eyes. It was surely the same sadness she felt when her clients left her, with no promise of return, no hint of affection. She had no doubt already seen what I was eyeing in the distance. A dismal form beckoning the hopeless to throw themselves into the sea. A deathly sign that was at times disguised as a release, a happy ending. Bijou had understood that I'd wanted to cast myself into the water not to drown, but to reach another world where I'd be given a chance.

What prompted our lovemaking on the beach was that we both wanted to leave. We were both obsessed with living elsewhere, being happy somewhere. Bijou dispelled my suicidal thoughts, rekindled my extinguished hopes. She gave herself to me so that I could reach the hot and exciting life within her that was so repressed. She opened her thighs more nobly for me than for any white man. She arched her back much harder for me, especially since I didn't judge her for what she was doing. On the contrary, I imagined someone who would come and help her leave her misery far behind.

Bijou had lost her father, who had been a motorcycle taxi driver in Cotonou. Those *zémidjans*, as they were called, weren't really vehicles, but angels of death. Every day amid ominous roaring and suffocating fumes, they brought about death and devastation on the city's bumpy streets. Heads would hit the broken-up paving stones and split open in the high sun. Few survived those taxis, and Bijou's father was no exception, ending his days with his innards spilled. It happened in front of Place des Martyrs in the blazing sun. All that risk for so little money.

"You know," Bijou said to me one day, "there are three types of white clients. The type that pays really well and never asks questions. They're often Canadian or American businessmen. The type that pays just the right amount and asks me about myself to make our relations a bit more personal. They're Europeans. And then there's the type that screws too much and almost never pays. Unfortunately, they're the most common around here. They're Eastern Europeans or sailors on the Mediterranean."

She told me all this in a light-hearted tone. Her voice sounded like that of a great many young birds who had matured before their time—birds that didn't sing the same dreary old tune.

Bijou was never angry, bitter, or even disgusted when she talked about her clients. Far from it: they were the field in which she would track down her salvatory prey; they were the gold mine in which she would one day unearth the finest vein ever seen. A wealthy white man in love with her. How many times she described the scene of her rise to the realm of the rich. The *yovo*, the white man, would swoon over her sweet little face and tremendous physique. Bijou spoke of her clientele as sacred material full of promise for her future.

I'd like to take this opportunity to get a message out to fans of prostitutes. Bijou, whose real name is Catherine Maïmouna Dossou, her mother being Catholic and her father Muslim, lives in Cotonou. I'm asking white men who are passing through Benin to go and see Bijou. It's not that other races or the feminine gender wouldn't do. It's just that with a white man, Bijou would never regret not setting her sights high enough. My goal is to find someone for Bijou who would take her away from these shores. Need I remind you that in the country where she lives, as in many other parts of Africa, it's difficult to find a way out? To blossom, people often wait for a miracle like a second birth. In almost all cases, nothing happens. However paradoxical, Bijou is confined to her beach in case a client comes along and happens to free her from this coast. There's no need to feel too sorry for her though, because love is unexpected and unpredictable. Often, people give themselves to the last person they would've thought they could love.

Bijou adores strolling by the water, eating vanilla ice, and going to nightclubs. An expert in several positions, she readily goes along with the most extreme fantasies. She wants to marry a *yovo* or even live with one, settle abroad, and have beautiful biracial children.

To see her during the week, simply walk along the beach at the Sheraton Hotel as far as the French school, then sit down and count the coconut trees. She'll come. On weekends, you'll find her at the Sheraton nightclub. She's easy to spot. She never wears a bra over that bountiful bosom.

Reminiscence of Failed Love

B ijou had always occupied my thoughts, even when I was an adolescent. I'd see her every weekend on the arm of a man, a different one each time. She was barely out of puberty and already a radiant beauty. Her velvety skin glowed with the shimmer of ripe fruit. Her light footsteps dug into the moist sand by the sea, and I dreamt of being the water that wet her ankles.

One weekend, I accompanied some fishermen out to the open sea. We left at dawn, even though the water had not completely calmed down from the turbulent night before. I went aboard not to fish, but to count the catch. The only fisherman able to do that job was in bed with severe malaria. The small boats the men used to fish were in no way reassuring. They were old pirogues, made of flimsy wood, and lacked stability. The paint on them, once brightly coloured to be visible from afar, had faded from the beating of the salty waves. On our pirogue, the words "God is Great" appeared in thick white paint.

A few minutes before I climbed aboard, I saw Bijou, her head on the shoulder of a white man with grey hair. He was slim, svelte. His features revealed hours of festivity and pleasure. His black jacket and his tie were fluttering in the morning breeze. I felt a sort of jealousy rise in me. I would've liked to be in his place, to hold Bijou by the arm. I couldn't stop staring at the carefree couple. Nothing seemed to exist beyond them. Bijou had eyes only for her knight, whose weariness had a certain charm.

A boy wearing a khaki uniform went up to the lovers. They stopped and listened to what the scrawny-legged child had to say. He was gesticulating, his brown knapsack, a small satchel of worn leather, shaking with his movements. He set his bag down at his feet and, without another word, climbed up a coconut tree with disconcerting agility. His big famished eyes chose one of the fruits. Shaking it hard, he managed to detach it. He let it fall and scrambled down the tree. Then he drew a rusty machete out of his satchel, placed the coconut between his legs, and went about splitting it with unexpected strength. The strength of hunger.

Meanwhile, Bijou had gone and sat down not far from there. She was holding her hair firmly with one hand because the breeze was picking up. Her evening dress clung to her skin, and I could imagine her breasts, under the light fabric, iridescent with the cool ocean spray. I couldn't see her eyes, but I guessed from the taut nape of her neck that she was impatient for her man of the day to return to her. The man rummaged through his pocket and rewarded the little boy, who disappeared like a shot.

The fishermen and I left almost immediately afterwards. I felt like going back to the shore, even if I had to swim. I wanted to tell Bijou that she was wasting her time with that man. But who was I? Why would she listen to me? I despised all her clients and imagined drowning them out at sea. They had what I could never have to win her over: white skin. Even if I'd been rich, she would've never seen in me what she sought in vain in white men. A type of life insurance, something to do with continuity, stability and, above all, power. A black man who has that is always afraid of losing it.

The calmness of the open sea brought me back to gentler thoughts. I remembered tender, unforgettable moments. I recalled the taste of a kiss I stole when Maïmouna was sleeping at her mother's house, and her cool hand on my feverish forehead covered with swollen beads of sweat. Then there was the time I held her by the waist when she was trying to make her way home, drunk.

Bijou seemed very close to me at that point. She was certainly with me on that trip. Raising my hand up to the sky, I hoped to touch her glistening hair. Unfortunately, she faded away and the sun's merciless rays beat down on my head.

The day before I was leaving for Toronto, I went to say goodbye to Bijou. I was shown to her room. That was the first time I'd had access to such a private place in her mother's house. I realized how much my departure gave me privileges. The room was bathed in dimness. A single bulb, timid and feeble, was trying to illuminate as many spots as possible. It cast a yellowish beam over an old dressing table.

I could make out Bijou's seated silhouette. There was a narrow bed, which reminded me of a cot. I was sure that my friend didn't bring any of her clients here. A vague smell of incense wafted through the room in hazy, fleeting swirls. As I made my way over to Bijou, I noticed that numerous postcards had been neatly put up, to decorate the room with a wall of images. Bijou's posture revealed the weight of her apprehension about my visit, my last visit. Everything seemed to have been prepared for me. Her appearance, her smile, her perfectly tidy room where I was allowed to see the main things, but not the misery. It's true that the misery of a place should never count in a farewell scene.

Bijou's dark and terribly round eyes looked like two spheres that had lost their centre of gravity that night. Yet she wore a smile full of self-confidence. She asked me to sit down, which I did for a minute. Then she broke into feigned laughter, telling me that she'd finally found her *yovo* and that she expected they'd soon be leaving for Europe. Her story was vivid and exciting, her voice full of conviction. She assured me that it would be pointless to write to her in Cotonou. She'd no longer be there to receive my letters.

The light in the room was constantly struggling with her gesturing shadow. She spoke so exuberantly that she didn't seem sincere to me. Her shadow betrayed the panic my departure was causing her. I sensed her contained anger—anger at remaining by those shores when I was leaving. But out of cowardice, I didn't want to talk about it. I already felt guilty for going, for leaving her behind, alone. Without her lie, she would've never been able to say a last goodbye. And I wouldn't have been able to look her in the eye. All I keep with me from the day we parted is her full presence there before me. The feel of her beautiful skin, soft and cool. Our last embrace amid the half-light, shimmering like the tears in our eyes.

Yonge Street Was First a Postcard

Yonge is the longest street in Toronto. Some people say it's the longest in the world. I'd known about Yonge well before I was able to stroll down it. I had a postcard featuring the street by night that Eddy had sent me when he was still writing to me. I'd put it up right in front of my bed. The image showed multicoloured car lights, which looked like shimmering emeralds on an endless runway. I'd often gaze at the pedestrians in it as well: passersby caught on the fly, multiple iterations of their blurry silhouettes creating a lively and electrifying atmosphere; night owls who had become veritable swirling souls radiating their energy to the surrounding streetlamps. The photo exuded so much vigour, evoked so many dreams, that Yonge Street became a dazzling, sparkling centre of activity in my mind, a place both sovereign and possessed.

So I spent my first morning in Toronto on Yonge Street. I must say that my feet took me there without too much trouble. I rode the bus on my own, with absolutely no knowledge of the city. After following a few directions from the driver, I was finally able to lay my eyes on the street that had long been on my mind.

Travelled by countless vehicles in every direction, Yonge Street stretched out like a reptile whose length reflected perpetual growth. Along its sidewalks, crowds moved, pulsated, and milled tirelessly about like ants around their egg-laying queen. What new life emerged before my eyes that day. What a revelation, what a discovery of races, colours, and well-stocked windows. Yonge Street alternated between clean, miserable, and grotesque, depending on the corner. It was decaying in some places and gleaming in others.

Walking down toward Lake Ontario from the intersection with Bloor, I was struck with a naive and childish fear of seeing myself merge into opaque lamplight, like the pedestrians on my postcard. The feeling lasted only a fraction of a second, but my heart leapt and, at the same time, I longed to be immortalized in the photo. Soon, I felt like imitating Yonge Street's singular rhythm. My ears were picking up thousands of syncopated steps—the brisk and spirited pace of colourfully dressed pedestrians, the discordant beat of footfalls, connected for better or worse with the cosmopolitan city. Passersby coming from all different backgrounds were brushing against each other in an improvised, jazzy way. And all these souls constantly coming and going were aware of one other in the heart of the city.

The throng eddied around all sorts of shops. The most luxurious jewellery stores stood alongside adult video outlets. Secondhand dealers hawked goods in front of high-end clothing boutiques. Pornographic magazines were sold beside a very popular and chaste New Age church. For sellers, Yonge Street was a constant battlefield. They had to be able to stand their ground and control their zone for as long as possible. Their informal hunt for buyers turned all pedestrians into potential prey. Nowhere else would a prospective customer be pursued more than here. If people didn't go into a shop, they were caught outside by some smooth-talking or seductive salesperson. Then there were the countless flyers and leaflets that wound up in the hands of those walking by.

Yonge Street was entrancing because of its market-driven hustle and bustle. This was my first real experience as a consumer, and I was not up to the task. The street made me long for things that I could not yet possess.

Heading back to the apartment, I got onto a bus. The atmosphere on it was grim, the faces of the passengers closed and vacant. Yet people were giving each other the eye here and there out of curiosity. The driver, short and fat, appeared as indifferent as possible. Amid the banging and hissing of the automatic doors, riders were trying to read newspapers, which they folded and unfolded while fidgeting in their seats as if being watched. I let myself be fascinated once again by the clothes, movements, and affected appearance of those around me. Everything seemed grander than usual: berets worn at an angle by the consciously eccentric, sneakers with immensely long laces, and even ties made of a satiny material.

It being summer, I had a chance to gaze at the half-naked bodies of the sun worshippers among them. Their barely-covered round buttocks and muscular thighs were lasciviously revealed. Despite my admiration for their physical fitness, I had a questioning gleam in my eyes. Why would anyone surrender personality in order to show off a beautiful body, even if only for a few hours? It intrigued me. These scantily clad people were sure of beating old age, defeating impotence, and prevailing over life. They embodied, according to their values, an undeniable form of desire and sensuality. The importance they placed on their physiques and on exposing them reflected a certain freedom, in a rebellious and smug sense.

The partial nudity I'd known was often so unintentional that this display of skin dumbfounded me. I remembered the gnarled torsos and bulging muscles of cart pushers drenched with sweat in the scorching heat. Hardly clothed, they pushed from morning to night, their chests protruding, their arms tensed, their calves thin and veiny from hauling monstrously heavy goods for kilometres. Despite their suffering, I couldn't help but be captivated by their bodies, soaked from all the strain. I recalled women merchants sweltering in stalls at the Dantokpa Market, wearing only bras on top so they wouldn't suffocate from the heat. There, the slippery, sticky skin exposed was linked to hard work, the constant striving to eke out a living. On the bus, people bared their skin arrogantly and freely just to defy life.

When I got to the subway, I had to ride down the escalator. I wasn't used to those moving stairs. The steel steps appearing one after the other from beneath the floor made me reel. The crowd behind me prevented me from turning back and regaining my balance. So I clutched the handrail and lurched onto a step on the left. People were walking down around me, glancing at me, annoyed. I assumed that they understood I lacked experience on revolving stairs. I was on the side where people passed, but I didn't know anything about that. By the time I realized what was going on, it was too late. I'd reached the bottom. I felt very uncomfortable, so primitive in the face of progress. Of course, this wasn't the first time I'd thought myself inferior, but here I felt like a member of a unique species, far away from blacks like me. The reason I blundered on the escalator, a machine so common in the West, was because people in the poor place I'd come from were unfamiliar with modern innovations.

In Toronto, I didn't have a majority with which to compare myself to justify my actions. I was alone. Even the other black faces were just that and nothing more. I knew that I had to stop belittling myself. But to get rid of my unwarranted admiration for white people, I had to get to the bottom of the myth. I had to delve deeply into its mystery, if I was to emerge satisfied and healed one day. I saw this struggle with my own demons as a longer and much more perilous journey than the one I'd taken to get to Toronto. Yet I was willing to risk my soul, my whole life, to defeat my inner monsters.

The Subway

The subway is a metallic snake that chases its own shadow within the bowels of the earth. The underground in Toronto is filled with thousands of other deceptive shadows. I was waiting on the platform when my train appeared in the tunnel amid yellowish lights that cast a sickly gloss along the sides of the cars. I noticed how slowly the train seemed to be travelling, as if it was having difficulty pulling out of the obscure horizon. When it finally rolled past me, circled by a strong hot wind, I realized how quickly it was moving. It came to a stop, opened its doors, and let out its human tentacles like a carnivorous monster, a prince of darkness. When it started again, people had to hang on, to withstand the jolting. It rushed into the blackness amid strident braking, rounded bends in a nocturnal labyrinth, and made timed stops there. In my car, everything was shaking fiercely, and I had trouble eluding the elbows of the other passengers. They appeared utterly indifferent, the telluric forces apparently no longer having any effect on them. Surely this underground confinement, this untimely interment, had some impact on these people with impassive faces. In this place, you had to keep your spirit in check to prevent terror from overcoming your mind. At each stop, short sharp cues rang out—the rigid authority that directed the train without completely controlling it, the voice of the intercessor between us and the devil. The martial tone told us what to do, so as to avoid ending up in eternal ruins. Despite my fear, I felt exhilarated in this incessant urban noise. I had the sensation of floating in a new liquid as intoxicating as alcohol. This subterranean world imprinted on my iridescent senses the mark of a rough and ruthless city, but one so thrilling.

At the station exit-entrance, I saw subway employees behind large windows in their ticket booths, ensuring that users paid their fares. They were sitting right there in front of customers, who were at the mercy of their condemning gazes. Once outside, I sat down on a public bench and closed my eyes. I could still see the bright colours of all the merchandise in the windows on Yonge Street. I could see skyscrapers thrusting fiercely through wispy white summer clouds in an absurd and vertiginous coital act.

I walked from the subway back to the apartment, shivering somewhat. My faded old shirt was worn and drafty. The frayed edges reminded me of my Sundays of washing by hand. I did laundry for clients, and sang as I went along, to make the time pass quickly. I had determination and a large rectangular bar of soap that was more or less grey. I worked around a well that left something to be desired. The water was not very clear and, more importantly, it was a breeding ground for mosquitoes. I had to stop thinking about that, though. I had to walk to the apartment and rid my mind of those days when happiness was impossible.

Back in North York

That evening, Joseph seemed to be in a very good mood. He was humming tunes from his native Haiti while preparing dinner. Bob, his friend with the dreadlocks, was strumming his all-black guitar, following Joseph's lead. When I walked into the kitchen, Bob glanced up through his ringlets. We were the only ones in the apartment since my roommate, Koffi, wasn't home yet. After we greeted each other, I sat down with them. I listened to them sing for a little while, then I asked Bob,

"Where are you from exactly?"

He didn't stop playing. I could feel something different in his posture, something tense. I couldn't see his eyes, which were lowered on his guitar, but I could certainly imagine the animosity lodged in them. He eventually looked up at me, his eyes glowing with hostility.

"I'm from Jamaica, but I grew up in Detroit. I'm a Jamaican from Detroit, okay?" he said, in a snide tone.

He immersed himself in his music again. I realized that I got on his nerves. I wanted to try and change his attitude toward me.

"What do you do for a living?"

"I'm a musician."

He continued strumming the tune that Joseph had stopped singing. His fingers slid on the strings with great agility. "I play the blues," he continued proudly, "soul, jazz, reggae, calypso. I stir the black soul with the sounds it created."

As Bob spoke, I stared at the bracelets on his strong wrists. They clinked every time he moved his hands and provided a pleasing accompaniment to his guitar. Bob was the most reserved of my hosts. The palms of his black hands were somber, his fate lines running into disconcerting gloom. He took a puff of the cigarette he'd left in the ashtray in front of him.

"Why are you asking me Babylon questions?"

When I didn't answer, he added, "You're African and you talk like a white man. What else do you want to know about me? If I like Greek restaurants? In what neighborhood I'm going to buy a house?"

He shook his head in disapproval. "Those aren't questions for us. That's Babylon talk. The type of thing the people who govern us say."

His small gleaming eyes disappeared in a puff of smoke. Without waiting for my reaction, he started playing "Redemption Song" by Bob Marley, as if to make his point. Joseph immediately joined him with his warm voice.

From the way they sang, I could see their symbiosis, their harmony, which kept me out of their duo. The cohesion of their voices was exceptional, and I gradually went from being a spectator to an intruder. I felt like the sole lost link in a chain forever broken. The lyrics of the song evoked the suffering of the slaves and the courage of contemporary blacks. Bob and Joseph were conveying their emotions to me, arousing a feeling of guilt in me, even though I had the same colour of skin. It showed me that I couldn't identify with them. They were well aware of it. I was discovering it, to my amazement. But I couldn't manage to put myself in their shoes and sympathize with them like any other stranger. Their history made them inaccessible. I couldn't reach them in any way. They had the barrier of centuries around them, centuries spent far from Africa where everything that had happened to them was like nothing else.

When Bob and Joseph finished their song, I clapped for a long time, trying to show them how much they'd moved me. They merely congratulated each other.

During dinner, they exchanged anecdotes. I listened without understanding what they were talking about or sharing their enjoyment. I thought that I'd eventually get to know them better and that my feeling of being an outsider would disappear.

The sun didn't set until so late in summer that I wondered if there was something magical behind it. After all, in Cotonou, on the days that big soccer games were held, people asked the gods to make sure the sun would keep on shining.

Tarzan Didn't Come from Africa

B ob and Joseph were still absorbed in conversation, so I decided to watch television. In Cotonou, there was only one channel on TV. Here, it was impossible to count them all. The colours of the picture were brighter and more attractive. The commercials, which interrupted programs with systematic regularity, were full of humour and featured all kinds of stories. I'd never seen such vitality. The screen looked like an animated object with electrifying images. I realized, however, that I hadn't seen the same vibrant atmosphere on the way to the apartment. The high-rise where I was staying didn't have the sparkling futuristic look of the buildings on television. There were no grey suburbs or dimly lit corridors on TV, only a fabulous world where people could have anything money could buy. The wobbly armchair in which I was sitting seemed like a trap. The arms felt as if they were trying to close in on me. I fought back my dark thoughts by watching television more attentively. I wanted to get away from it all, and *The Adventures of Tarzan* was on. Tarzan was a white man with long blond hair. His best friend was a monkey practically endowed with the ability to speak. The blacks that Tarzan was commanding were almost naked. Some were wearing kinky wigs and others, with wrathful eyes, were attacking a motionless vehicle as if it were a dangerous person or animal. The images seemed unconvincing to me. Yet the scene was taking place in Africa. I didn't feel targeted, let alone disparaged. I was simply watching a film by an oddball screenwriter.

During this time, Bob and Joseph had been continuing their conversation. Suddenly, Bob turned around and switched off the television, swearing. Then the two of them resumed their discussion with new intensity. Once again, I realized how different we were. I didn't react like Bob because I didn't have anything against the white American who wrote the story. The film, as degrading as it might be, wasn't about me. It was close to absurd and far from insulting. There weren't any colonists or colonized people, just primitives obeying a white man barely clothed himself. It was a North American myth. Tarzan didn't come from Africa. He was a product of the Western imagination. My hosts and I weren't in the same war. I found this realization discouraging.

Joseph Dorsinville's Story

Joseph was born in Gonaïves, but he grew up in the capital, Port-au-Prince. He didn't remember much about his hometown: just the abundance of black pigs, the scraggy vegetation, and the eroding hills. He thought that the man who had raised him was not his real father. He was convinced that his biological father was one of those *brasseros* or sugarcane cutters who left the country to work in the Dominican Republic for next to nothing. Joseph's belief that he was the son of one of those modern-day slaves seemed to awaken thinly-veiled pride in him. His brown eyes took on a dark hue as he talked about himself. Sitting in one of the armchairs in the living room, he asked Bob and me to stop doing the dishes and listen to what he had to tell us.

He'd left Haiti a number of years earlier and clearly remembered the time when he was working as an orderly at a private clinic in Port-au-Prince. His stepfather had moved heaven and earth to land him that job. One evening as he was leaving a room, a young biracial woman fell at his feet, gasping for breath. He hadn't seen her coming and wondered how on earth she got there. Her face pale and her clothes blood-soaked, she seemed to be begging him for help. Her grey eyes rested on him for a few seconds, flickered, then she passed out. While Joseph was checking that she was still alive, he heard authoritative voices just beyond the hallway.

"Where is she?"

"Which way did she go?"

Joseph, acting in panic, decided that he had to hide her.

"I didn't have much time to think . . . ," he said. "And those grey eyes, right there in front of me. I couldn't leave her."

He wrapped the woman in a blanket on a bed that was in the hallway. Then he headed toward her pursuers, as if nothing had happened. When two soldiers appeared in the hallway, he pointed them in the wrong direction and told them the woman had gone that way.

"It was later," he continued, "when they took her to the operating room, that I found out she was the daughter of a senior army officer, a drug baron in Haiti. She pulled through."

Joseph spoke with a sort of tenderness in his voice, as if wanting to soothe some old sorrow with his warm intoning.

"Why was she being chased?"

At first, he said he didn't really know. Then he changed his mind.

"There was a rumour going around Port-au-Prince that her father was furious when he found out she was sleeping with a Haitian painter instead of studying at Yale. Apparently, the guy was singing for a living in the seedy neighbourhoods of Brooklyn."

Joseph paused for a moment, then said, "Her father shot her!"

"What?"

I couldn't believe what he was telling us. He explained that Véronique had humiliated her father by going out with a man who was not only penniless, but black.

"Biracial people are biracial. You can't get one of their daughters just any old way."

I didn't think he was telling us this story just to talk about the tacit laws of Haitian lords. So I kept quiet and continued listening. Joseph ran his hands absentmindedly over his face.

"The soldiers came back the next day. If Véronique hadn't regained consciousness and intervened on my behalf, I wouldn't be here tonight. The employees at the clinic advised me to leave. They told me I was lucky that time, but that Véronique might not be there the next. I sent word to her that I wanted to get out of the country. She got me a student visa for Canada the next day, to thank me for what I'd done. I got a telex from her yesterday. She's coming to Toronto to visit some cousins soon. She'd really like to see me."

After a long silence, Bob remarked, "Well, there aren't degrees of blackness here. Either you're black or you're not. That woman isn't coming to see her family. She's coming to see you, man! Don't miss this chance . . . You have to blacken her!" he said, smiling faintly.

Bob picked up his guitar with one hand and turned to Joseph, shaking his head. His dreadlocks swung so vigorously that they covered his face instantly.

"Poor Joe!"

That's what he called him, still wearing his ambiguous smile. Then he mumbled something barely comprehensible about going to bed.

Joseph took over doing the dishes with me, the rattling of the plates filling the void after Bob left. I thought how lucky Joseph was to have had a benefactress. And to think how many people would sell their souls to the devil to lay their hands on the visa he obtained.

"What did you do when you got here?" I asked, somewhat hesitantly.

Joseph looked at me.

"What? When I landed in Toronto?"

"Yes."

"Oh!" he said, plunging his hands into the soapy water. "I went to school and my life consisted of listening to people talk about their history, their view of how things happened, their poets. And I had to starve to do it."

He smiled ironically, adding, "I was in the History Department . . . Did you know that Canada's been celebrating black history for less than twenty years?"

Joseph glanced up at the ceiling, then swallowed painfully as if his saliva bore the weight of unforgettable centuries.

"I come from a country where it's important to get an education. You have to learn to speak French like a European, English like an American. My whole childhood, I admired those black teachers who came back from France or the United States . . . You had to come from somewhere else, not Haiti. But it wasn't until I got here that I understood how hypocritical their teaching was. All for the glorification of the West."

He stopped for a moment and asked me to fetch the cutlery left on the dining table. I brought it to him quickly so he'd continue.

"Of course, at first you don't actually realize it. You think you're smart enough to keep things in perspective. Then you start to admire people like Cromwell, Lord Durham, and Jacques Cartier, and you gradually understand that no one in your class has heard of Toussaint Louverture, Jean-Jacques Dessalines, or Lumumba. The worst part of it is that you unconsciously start to forget them, too. Little by little, you're no longer sure of the impact Martin Luther King had on the fate of humanity. So I left school before I forgot the importance of my history."

Joseph was so articulate that I could've easily thought this wasn't the first time he'd given such a speech. He hadn't learned to express himself so well by attending to bleeding patients at a posh clinic in Port-au-Prince. It had taken more than that. He had to have come from a fairly elite background to talk the way he did. I mean, he spoke French just as well as he did English. What concerned me at this point, though, was that he'd wanted to tell us something with his story about Véronique. I hadn't been able to grasp what it was.

"Why did you want to tell us about Véronique?"

Joseph smiled again. This time, there was a hint of sadness on his face. He dried the last of the glasses without a word, as if considering the reasons why he should answer me frankly.

"Well, I don't want Véronique to know that I'm not using my student visa anymore. She got it for me with good intentions."

Seeing my slightly confused look, Joseph added, "She wouldn't understand. She's the colour of honey syrup. As I said, biracial people in Haiti don't have the same problems as us. They're concerned about staying light-skinned and not becoming black. She thinks that education is the only solution for a black like me. When you control your country's economy, you don't have to be educated. History, geography, and physics are for the poor. What bothers me is that the girl really had my best interests at heart. But my happiness doesn't depend on anyone but me."

Joseph was standing in front of me, gesturing as he spoke. He looked as if he was grabbing invisible forms in space or giving a political speech before an entire audience.

"And now that she's coming here," I said in a tone intended to be neutral, "you don't know how to tell her that you've chucked your student visa."

Joseph didn't answer. He put the dishes away and went to sit down in the living room, looking pensive. I took his silence as affirmation. He'd no doubt kept in touch with Véronique and lied to her about what he was doing in Toronto. Maybe he'd told her that he'd achieved academic feats or something like that. The idea that someone living elsewhere might lie worried me. I wondered if Eddy had lied to me about what he was doing. Had he really become an actor as he'd said in his letters? Was he really doing television commercials? I didn't dare check with my hosts. If Eddy had lied to me, I wouldn't be able to take it. I was afraid someone would tell me that an immigrant in Toronto might have a hard time doing what he wanted to do in life. I suspected it. I could even say that I knew it. But I didn't want to hear it.

Joseph criticized Western education for its lack of objectivity. At the same time, he wanted Véronique to think of him as a good student. He was a prisoner of the values he condemned. Looking him in the eye, I was afraid of rousing my own contradictions—the contradictions of a colonized soul. It's true that I felt a certain pride in knowing Napoleon's main conquests. But I also spat on the emperor for plundering so many civilizations, including my own, for the glory of his country. That's the dilemma of the colonized.

Joseph offered me a beer, which I accepted.

The Westin Hotel

J oseph told me that he'd worked at the Westin Hotel in Toronto. It was an elegant place with a permanently revolving restaurant at the top. Most of the rooms had windows overlooking a lake dotted with islands, which reminded him of his homeland. Joseph had to wear a khaki uniform and a dark brown tie to work. His job was to stock the refrigerators, bill the guests, and replenish the minibars from a cart loaded to the hilt. He developed horrible back pain from bending over to check the inventory in the minibars. Given the large number of rooms he had to work in, he covered so much ground every day that it wasn't unusual for him to get blisters on his feet.

Joseph believed that the job was fit for an automaton. However, he took advantage of it as much as possible. He would spend long periods watching the sun disappear below the horizon, thinking about his native island. The view of the lake and the small islands was magnificent. Every now and then, he would take a shower in one of the empty rooms and stock up on soap, bath towels, and toilet tissue. When it came to drinks, he would guzzle any extra rum he could take from the liquor supply room in the hotel basement. He could access the minibars with his key and the rooms with a master key he wore around his neck. He would watch porn films on pay-per-view channels before the indicator light activated billing, or listen at the door of noisy lovers. Sometimes he would enter the room if the occupants had forgotten to lock it, pretending that he'd made a mistake.

Joseph went on about his escapades at the hotel for quite a while. I could see how much he relished the times he'd outwitted the system.

"Then one day, I'd had enough. And I left."

As he said this, he seemed to regain his usual good humour.

"And you? What did you do in Africa?"

I noticed a touch of derision in his suddenly cheerful expression.

Something that prevented him from taking me altogether seriously. I didn't know what it was exactly.

"Oh, not much . . . I helped people out here and there . . . I did a little sewing, a little ironing. I sold a few things on the black market."

"I see," he said in a friendly manner. "You got by. Are you married? Do you have any kids?"

"No. Not married. No kids."

"Oh well, here you'll have lots of choice!"

"Why do you say that?"

"Because the girls here aren't difficult. When they want you, they want you!"

I didn't like the turn the conversation was taking at all. He was anxious to ease the concerns of a little lost African in Toronto.

"Personally, I like women too much to ever get married," he declared. "Raymond, I dream about women every night. Always different ones from the night before. The women in Toronto are sexy!"

Joseph laughed, winking at me. His breath reeked of beer. I felt disgusted at the thought that I might smell as bad as him. His attitude was irritating me more and more. I didn't need a mentor or a matchmaker. Even if I did, I certainly wouldn't have chosen him. But he had the right to treat me like a novice, because I was new to Toronto.

"Where I come from," he continued, "we make love in silence. It's like when you dance a slow. You have to hold your girl tight and savour the dark. Here, it's all right to talk when you're getting it on. It's even encouraged. They're completely crazy," he said cheerfully.

Seeing that I merely smiled, he gave me a friendly slap on the back. He was proud of his little monologue, convinced that he was going to help me one way or another. He'd just done his duty as one black toward another, who hadn't heard it all before. He would've continued had he not noticed the cold glint in my eyes. I was grinning. In truth, I was furious.

Joseph couldn't contain himself. He ended up telling me about some of his "best lays." Then he dozed off under the effect of the beer.

White Women in Africa

I n Cotonou, white women were the sought-after flowers. You didn't go near them, though, even during a political crisis. They kept very busy tending to their glory and influence. White women didn't go just anywhere. They could be seen at the leading hotels, in upscale neighbourhoods, around the French lycée, and at Westernized nightclubs. They were often beautiful. And when they weren't, they made you think they were, by the way they dressed. Most of the time, they were the wife or daughter of a civil servant. Always at the hairdresser or the couturiere's, they also liked to lie in the sun. Surrounded by servants, they knew how to win respect. And respect very often led to admiration.

When I was a child, I'd watch the white women at the Dantokpa Market. They would park their cars, stay inside, and wait for the pack of black women who ran after vehicles to sell their goods. Then they'd keep their car windows rolled up quite high, so they could negotiate prices without being mobbed by a multitude of outstretched hands. After haggling with the merchants, to show that they weren't fresh off the boat from Europe, they'd open their purses, hold out some new bills, and wait for the change. Because of that, I long believed that white women's purses had something to do with the origin of money.

Had the white women in Cotonou ever dreamt of such a good life in their native countries? All those servants, all that respect went to their heads. They walked around like queens in their realms. They didn't really look at you: they stared at the goods they wanted to buy, or they waited for the service you were to provide. Their buying power was their main asset. They could dress better than many African women. Even if they didn't manage to all the time, you knew they were capable of it. That's what mattered. They had the means to buy you a drink at a chic restaurant, a simple drink for which you would've had to scrimp and save for three weeks. Some days, I would've given my soul for one of those drinks at the Croix du Sud, a fancy restaurant frequented by white women. There, my thirst was that of a guy ready to drink to the last drop everything that the darkness of a hotel room would have gotten him.

Sometimes I'd also prowl around the French Cultural Centre looking for that elusive drink. I'd watch those white ladies step outside during the intermission of their theatrical performance. They'd smoke their cigarettes with a distinguished air. They seemed lonely and vulnerable to me. I'd often try to look natural, carrying a book under my arm. And every cigarette tip that reddened in the night would light a white-hot spark deep in my chest. I kept hoping that a word or gesture would reach me and start a blinding, all-consuming fire. I was convinced that those blue, green, and grey eyes noticed my movements. I was sure that they were following me, like the last beacon in the storm of my life, the last chance.

Then the cigarettes would leave their lips and fall at their feet. They liked to crush them with their spike heels. After a small twist of their ankles, I'd return to total darkness, absolute darkness, which in reality I'd never left.

Back home, I'd feel ashamed of myself. Ashamed of such an awkward attempt to sell myself. And yet I would've bet that the next month, I'd be plagued by the same desperate thirst again.

Koffi, a Night Owl

Koffi came into the bedroom in the middle of the night, after leaving Joseph in the living room. He switched on the light and started talking to me.

"What's new?"

"Hmm . . ."

"Did you have a nice day?"

"Hmm yeah," I mumbled, still half asleep. "Not bad."

I wanted him to let me sleep off the beer. But he'd brought his cassette player in like the night before. His body looked gigantic in the small room and cast unsettling reflections on the walls. He rolled a joint with his thick fingers and lit it in silence. His slow gestures were like a ritual in a secret religion. After taking a long puff, his eyes closed, he handed me the joint and went to turn off the light. The cigarette between my fingers was so small that I almost burned myself like the previous night.

"You'll get used to it," said Koffi. "It takes time. At some point, you won't feel your fingers anymore."

He laughed softly in the darkness. I liked his throaty spontaneous laughter, which filled the room but was never imposing. He played another Bob Marley song, this one called "Zimbabwe."

When our eyes became accustomed to the dark, Koffi lifted his head, seeking my gaze.

"Brother, I don't understand why blacks can't get along with each other. Why don't we listen to the prophet who sings 'One Destiny'?"

Koffi wanted the joint back. I handed it to him without replying. I knew he wasn't really looking for an answer. It was the type of question you ask to lament the fate of your people. He continued talking about unity. I grunted in agreement from time to time.

The joint was quick to take effect, and I felt a tropical heat spread through me. It wasn't Bijou who I saw in my hazy thoughts that night, but Professor Pangloss, who was known as the "Death Defier." He was a learned man who, through his tragic fate, taught me about the fickle nature of life.

Pangloss Wasn't in His Right Mind

The former professor may not have been in his right mind, but that didn't detract from his qualities. The events causing this intellectual's descent into sheer madness were unclear to me. His past was engulfed by the same murkiness as his mind. People said he was from a noble family in Ghana which had settled in Cotonou before the professor was born. Pangloss had taken part in the "Marxist Revolution" in Benin. He was then sent as a diplomat to Eastern European countries and during that time apparently declined a chair at the University of Oxford for ideological reasons. It was abroad that he mysteriously lost his mind and had to be brought back to Cotonou immediately. The first time I met him, he had just left the hospital with no significant improvement in his condition. He would wander the city streets speaking French, English, and Russian to anyone who would listen. Saddled with the name "Pangloss" by his former students, without anyone really knowing why, he was nicknamed the "Death Defier" by the people of Cotonou because he crossed the streets with no concern for traffic. He wore a three-piece suit regardless of the heat. Although his clothing was faded, it retained the sobriety of Soviet cuts. Pangloss often gave long outdoor speeches to students interested in learning the art of politics and diplomacy. When he was alone, he would contemplate the statues in Place des Martyrs, smoking copiously and looking distinguished. Cigarettes were the only reward he would accept from his students.

I would go to see him and get him started on a political monologue, just to hear him speak. He would discuss crucial world events in which he'd participated. I was amazed by his oratory, which he'd learned from the Jesuit priests at Collège Aupiais—priests he had personally taken care of deporting during the "Marxist Revolution." As he talked, I would offer him a cigarette, trying to capture a moment of serenity in his eyes. But there would be nothing particular in his gaze. His fragile figure, however, which shuffled aimlessly about the streets, betrayed tremendous loneliness under the yoke of his tragic fate. He represented, in and of himself, an Africa that had been piously educated, that had revolted, and that was now obsolete. During his monologues, I could easily imagine him discussing politics with the great leaders of a bygone era. When he stopped, I would find him sitting there on the steps of Place des Martyrs in one of his ageless suits, and I would literally freeze with fear. The fickle nature of his fate, the alarming speed with which he'd gone from the red carpet to an urban stain, chilled my spine. I wanted to get away from Pangloss. I wanted to flee the inevitability that stuck to him and that gripped many destinies in the Third World. I left him promising myself that I'd never end up like him—receiving, as the only reward for services rendered, the ingratitude of his people.

I remembered one day in particular that I'd spent with Pangloss. For no apparent reason, he interrupted his monologue and stared intensely at an invisible object on the horizon. Then, his voice trembling, he cried out,

"Oh, Tatiana! You turned my whole life upside down. Do you remember when I went to get you at the national library in Moscow?"

The professor was looking at the statues in Place des Martyrs. Bewildered, I asked him who he was talking to.

"Why, to Tatiana Ivanovitch!" he shouted, utterly beside himself. "To that woman over there, with the green-blue eyes! The one clinging to the soldier!"

"Yes . . . um . . . Yes, I see her."

"You fool!" he bellowed. "She's already gone! White women don't just have cat eyes. They also have nine lives!"

Pangloss smiled for the first time since I'd known him. A smile that failed to conceal his deep-seated sorrow. Then, looking horribly ravaged by a dull, gnawing pain, he said almost in a murmur,

"I promised you the West, Tatiana. I promised you freedom . . . in a few months . . . freedom for you and me!"

He turned to the statues that valiantly represented the heroes of his country's revolution and cried out again, "Why did you plunge me into this darkness? Why?"

His voice was full of rage, his tone pleading. His feeble body was suddenly filled with new strength that seemed to rebel against his madness. He braced himself as if he were going to charge those huge inert stones with his entire body.

"Those sons of bitches threw me out! Those so-called comrades kicked me out of their country! They didn't want to know anything about love! Those bastards didn't want me to take you away!"

He collapsed on the dusty ground, his tears mingling with the infinite sands, his wounds mixing with the roots of the earth. His face distorted by harrowing grief, he still managed to say, "Look what they've done to me, Tatiana! Look!"

Then, still sobbing with the anguish that had long been eating away at his heart and mind, he picked up some stones and started hurling them at the indifferent statues. I tried to calm him down, but to no avail. Anger had taken hold of him. I ended up leaving him to his fate and disappeared into the crowd of onlookers that had formed.

I had discovered the heart of his madness, the nerve centre of his aimlessness. He was crushed by the hatred of man toward his fellow man. His Russian comrades had destroyed him at the peak of his career, at the height of his love for Tatiana. Because he had intended to betray his ideology for a Russian woman. He had affronted the fraternity of peoples by loving someone who wanted to be free. Unfortunately, he failed in his desire to free her.

Pangloss had lost everything and found himself shackled by a dead-end past. He never strayed far from the statues in Place des Martyrs because he hoped to get his revenge on history one day. He wanted those inert heroes to come to life one morning so that he could stone them to death for lying to him all those years about the fraternity of peoples. Every evening, Pangloss sank a little deeper into the bottomless sea of the night. A scrawny silhouette with shaggy hair, he was a volcano waiting to erupt. Waiting for the time when the last drop of love he possessed would join his streaming lava of hatred.

A Strange Woman in My Room

The next morning, after dreaming about Pangloss, I saw a stranger come into my room. She bent down and kissed me on the lips. Half asleep, I thought I'd drifted into another dream. When I opened my eyes, I jumped. The stranger burst out laughing and leaned over me again, to show me that she was quite real. Her chest became flushed. This time, I was sure that she was there before me, in the flesh.

"If you could see the look on your face," she said. "I'm not going to bite you, you know."

She left the room, and I heard her making some noise in the kitchen. At first, I just sat on the bed, completely baffled. Then I got up, hoping she hadn't mistaken me for someone else. I couldn't imagine that she would've kissed me instead of another man. But I still had my doubts. I thought it better to hold off meeting her by going to the bathroom.

I was in the shower, so I didn't hear the bathroom door open. The stranger appeared on the other side of the steamed-up glass and seemed to be making out the contours of my body under the spray of water. I couldn't quite manage to discern her gaze, but I could feel her desire coursing through me. I felt as if she stood there watching me for quite some time, and each second that passed seemed to clarify our intentions to be intimate. The young woman flipped her wavy black hair, a sort of pointless gesture at first glance, but one that became very seductive in light of our mutual attraction. I had trouble keeping my eyes open under the jet, but noticed her making as if to turn around and leave. My hand immediately opened the glass door then stopped, waiting for her reaction. She saw my body streaming with water; I beckoned her to come in. A smile on her lips, she undressed and joined me. Then the spray blurred my vision, and I couldn't see her totally naked. In the water raining down, I felt a pleasurable

sensation rising in my pelvis. I opened my eyes and caught sight of a
bare back, guitar-shaped hips, and arms wrapped around my buttocks.
I had to shut my eyes again because I kept getting water in them and
couldn't properly see what was going on. From time to time, despite
the stinging in my eyes, I glimpsed a woman lighting a fire in the
downpour, a woman with a firm back and my sex amid her dark wet
hair. I felt a heat languorously settling deep within me, my member
ablaze. The woman's movements were more nimble, less urgent than
those of Bijou. It wasn't about making love to escape despair. I was
discovering a whole playful intention to these caresses in the water.
The stranger was sliding her tongue over my shaft with feigned indifference. Although my eyes were closed, I could imagine her keeping
a tight rein on her passion as if subduing a tiger. Without seeing her,
I could feel how skilfully she drew her tongue over my member, wet-
ting and swelling every vein. Then she planted a chaste kiss on my tip
and slowly rose to her feet. Our eyes met, glowing with desire. With
an agile movement, she brought my sex into the rivulet between her
thighs. Still slowly, almost gently, she took me into her depths without so much as a murmur. The sparks she lit in me made me forget
that I was in water. The droplets became thousands of caresses and
their shushing grew more and more faint in my mind. Little by little, I
felt myself nearing the pinnacle. As my pleasure climbed, I saw myself
within the loins of all the white women in Cotonou, all the women in
the world. I was experiencing exhilaration and ecstasy in new waters,
in the arms of a stranger who represented everything that was inaccessible to me.

Still in the haze of pleasure, four words came furtively to mind. My
lips still wet, I murmured, "Toronto, I love you."

After the shower, the young woman whispered,
   "I'm Maria."
   She dressed as quickly as she'd removed her clothes.
   "I'm Raymond."
   "I know," she said smiling. "Joseph told me about you. You're Eddy's

friend from Africa."

She was silent for a few seconds, watching my expression, then exploded with laughter.

"If Joseph could see you now," she said. "I can tell by the look on your face that this is the first time you've made love with a stranger."

As she was leaving the bathroom, she stopped and leaned against the door frame.

"Don't worry . . . No one in this apartment is going to find out what happened . . . I promise," she said, stifling her laughter. "It's none of their business. My life is mine and mine alone," she added, suddenly serious.

She disappeared down the hall. I heard her footfalls leave the apartment and the door close. Her steps echoed all through the corridor and reached me like fierce, unexpected waves. I was dumbstruck, cursing the fact that this woman could read me so easily. But I was also delighted, because it meant that she knew I didn't regret anything.

When Maria returned, I was eating breakfast alone in the deserted apartment. She carried bags full of groceries into the kitchen, set them down on the floor, and started putting the food in the refrigerator. She turned to me, and we looked at each other for quite some time without a word. Lowering her dark eyes, she sighed loudly as if surrendering to an inner struggle.

"Okay, what do you want to know? If I'm Joseph's girlfriend? Or someone else's? Is that it? Go ahead," she urged, suddenly irritated, "ask me your questions!"

"But . . ."

"Oh! Now don't go trying to tell me that you haven't wondered who I'm with. Come on, I'm waiting," she continued, straightening up with a menacing look.

I didn't want to admit it to her, but I had actually wondered if she was going out with one of my roommates. I knew that if she was, it would be better for me not to know. I set my coffee down and gave her a questioning look. She smiled, appreciating my unspoken yet clear admission. She was standing in a ray of sunlight that had blossomed in her dark hair, a ray searching for the secret of her beauty. Her shining eyes didn't prevent me from also admiring her pendant earrings, which were catching the light and seemed to transform it into barely audible jingling. Maria was obviously waiting for me to say something. To avoid disappointing her, I asked,

"Are you one of Joseph's girlfriends' sisters?"

"No."

"Are you one of Joseph's co-workers?"

She didn't say anything but I could tell that she was holding back her laughter again. We looked at each other in silence for a few seconds, and she smiled at me. I smiled back. I wasn't too sure why we were smiling. I didn't want to spoil the moment, so I didn't ask her anything else.

"Listen, you seem like a nice guy . . . Anyway, you screw okay."

On this point, there was more silence, this time short-lived, then we both laughed. Trying to be serious again, she explained,

"Joseph's my ex. Oh, it's been over for a long time, but he's a good friend. I went out with a bunch of other guys after him. Then I started drinking and doing coke. Joseph was there to help me when I was in one hell of a mess."

Maria looked pensive. She opened her purse and pulled out a package of cigarettes.

"I help him out occasionally," she said in an amused tone, pointing to the food not yet put away.

I was amazed that she told me all this. After all, she barely knew me. But having showered together no doubt made it easier. Her troubles didn't seem to have hurt her. She was full of charm. And, as I was coming to understand, her mood could change in a flash. She spoke with enthusiasm, only her posture betraying a certain febrility.

"How did you meet Joseph?"

"I met him at a bar," she replied, slowly running her hands through her hair. "I see that he hasn't told you much."

Maria smoked nonchalantly, the front of her wrist outward, her fingers barely holding her cigarette.

"No, he hasn't told me anything. Well, he did tell me about a hotel by a lake the other day."

"Oh, yeah, the Westin Hotel. That was later on. I didn't meet him at a hotel. I met him at a seedy bar on Dundas West. I was living with some girlfriends at the time, flat broke. I'd had a falling-out with my parents . . . You know, teen crises, generational conflicts . . . A lot of shit."

Maria started putting away the rest of her groceries as she spoke.

"I was sitting at the bar with one of my girlfriends and this guy came over. I knew that someone had been watching me for quite a while. But in those days, I was high all the time. And when you're high, you don't really care who's looking at you . . . you have so many images going through your mind . . . Long story short," she continued, taking a puff of her cigarette, "the guy asked me to dance. To me, he wasn't just any guy. He was the first black guy. The first black guy in my life who asked me to dance. You must think that's ridiculous. But you have to understand that my mother always told me to stay away from black men. She said that they smelled like pot, they were dirty and, above all . . . they had big dicks! Of course, I knew it was all bull, but I'd always avoided them to make her happy. That night, I was totally wasted. I wasn't living at home anymore, so I thought, why not? I'll see if all the crap my mother was telling me had any truth to it, especially the part about the dicks! We danced three slows in a row, rubbing up against each other like crazy. But Joseph never tried to take me home with him. Much later on, when we knew each other better, I asked him why he hadn't tried. You know what he said?"

"No."

"He said that he never had a white woman get in his car after midnight."

"Why?"

"Apparently the cops think that a black guy in a car after midnight is suspicious. And with a white woman, you'll get stopped every time. At least the cops wait until midnight. My mother doesn't wait for anything. She thinks black men are suspicious all the time."

Maria started to laugh, and I smiled out of politeness. She lowered her head and waved away the smoke above her, as if to dispel what she'd just said. She went and stubbed her cigarette out in the sink, then looked at me out of the corner of her eye. I didn't hold her mother's prejudices against her. She'd wanted to talk about her mother, through her story about how she'd met Joseph.

"Where are you from exactly?"

She asked the question to change the subject. I could see that she wasn't really interested in where I was from. She wanted to draw me out, give me an excuse to talk about myself. I was too afraid to do so. I didn't want to reveal myself. So, I located Benin on an imaginary map for her and described some tourist attractions in Cotonou. I didn't mention the jobs I'd done there or the thousands of hours I'd spent on the beach dreaming of being somewhere far away. I thought she had to like Cotonou to be able to like me. I'd somehow gotten it into my head that, to make a good impression, it was better to embellish the place you came from.

Maria didn't make any comment about Cotonou. She didn't believe me.

"Why did you come here, then?" she ended up asking.

I didn't know what to say. I felt terribly ashamed.

"You're right, I haven't been telling you the truth. I did anything I could to survive back there."

"Anything?" she asked, wide-eyed.

"Almost anything."

"Why? Isn't there any work?"

"There isn't any money. The poor stay poor unless they steal. The rich stay rich because they steal."

"Why did you lie to me?" she asked, frowning.

"I guess I wanted you to respect me."

Maria remained impassive. My description of Cotonou was like a poisoned arrow with which I'd unwittingly shot myself. I said nothing else, embarrassed about being caught in the act. In view of my sudden silence, Maria smiled at me politely. She still had no idea where I was from. It's very difficult to explain to someone where you grew up.

Because, beyond the geographic place, there's the value of the life you led there. Life isn't an inert piece of land. It's pulsing with joy, filled with sadness. It's brimming with happiness, full of terror. To explain where you come from is also to talk about those you love, those you left behind who haunt you with their heartrending tune of absence and abandonment. It was impossible for me to tell her so quickly and in so few words where I'd come from.

"I'd like to know one thing," I said, out of curiosity.

"Yes? What?"

"Was it Joseph who told you to . . . um . . . "

"To make love with you? Oh, why won't guys understand that a woman can screw any man when she feels like it? Can you explain that to me?"

She fiddled with the many bracelets on her wrists. I could see that she was suppressing her anger. Then in a feigned calm but snide tone, she commented, "Oh, here's another one who thinks that all women are whores and that men are their pimps."

"That's not what I meant," I said, feeling awkward.

"What did you mean, then?"

Maria forced a smile. She got to her feet and gave me a murderous look.

"You'd better not say anything else, Raymond. You've surely never met women who were free to do what they wanted. With everything you see on TV, women with veils and all the rest of it. Bah! We still have a long way to go."

She picked up her purse.

"You coming?"

"Where?"

"I'd like to show you the city. Toronto's a liberated woman, too."

When Maria asked me to join her, she wasn't angry anymore. She'd already found her smile again.

The Pious Maria

Outside, Finch Avenue was bathed in radiant light, enhanced by the incomparable gilding of the sun. A joyous atmosphere extended over the entire suburban landscape. Scattered sunbeams were shining down on the parking lot. Maria led me to her red Corvette, casually opened the passenger's door for me, and walked around the car to open her own. Tenants were watching us from their balconies and some had no qualms about whistling in our direction.

"So how does it feel to be driven by a woman?" asked Maria, with a wink.

I didn't reply. I knew she was paying me back for the question I shouldn't have asked about Joseph. She winked at me again, this time in a more friendly way. Then she stuck her head out the window and shouted at the people on the balconies,

"Mind your own business!"

That set off even more whistling. Profanities burst forth like fireworks. Maria exploded with laughter, roared off, and honked many times. Her tires screeched and we disappeared round the corner. In the car, she continued to tell me about herself. Her parents arrived here from Portugal in the nineteen seventies. For her, until her late teens, Portugal was a sort of promised land. She spent her entire childhood celebrating the country's religious and national holidays. After a trip there to meet her family, somewhere in the countryside, she changed her mind about her parents' homeland. She got the shock of her life when she saw the poverty. She understood that Portugal wasn't just about holy water and folk dances. There was also a lack of running water and a lot of black bread. Maria thought that she'd turned to alcohol and drugs when she got home because she was so shaken by what she'd seen.

"I'd lost all sense of my values. I didn't know who I was anymore.

Joseph got fed up with seeing me high all the time. So he dragged me to an expert. To this day, I don't know how he paid for it. Little by little, with help, I was able to pull myself together. School's really enabled me to settle down. I'm studying psychology part-time at the University of Toronto. I want to specialize in support for abused kids."

"Do you still feel Portuguese?"

"Of course!" she replied, without hesitation. "But Portuguese from Toronto. There are still things to be kept from Portugal."

"Like what?"

"Like the faith. Speaking of which, I'm in charge of a children's church choir in the Portuguese neighbourhood."

I had difficulty imagining Maria as a believer. It seemed to me that her behaviour didn't attest to her faith in the Everlasting. I was used to believers who lowered their eyes all the time and talked about God as a light from heaven. I didn't think I'd made love with a pious woman.

"Yes! I believe in God," she insisted, seeing my stunned expression. "Maybe I'm going to hell, but I truly believe in God," she repeated, making the sign of the cross while touching a small pendant in her bodice.

I had a very hard time taking her seriously. But Maria was being sincere. To find harmony in her life, she was trying to reconcile her freedom as a woman with the values of her family's homeland. She was both of her generation in North America and of another in Europe. Her harmony had to be contradictory to exist.

Maria had other surprises in store for me. She announced that she'd been living with her parents since they'd settled their differences.

"When we made peace, I realized that I was their only child and that it broke their hearts to see me leave."

She didn't feel uncomfortable telling me about this aspect of her life. Everything seemed natural for her.

"I have to go and pick up someone's mail at my house."

Maria jerked her head toward me.

"You don't mind if we stop by my place, do you?"

"No, not at all."

Maria's Father

Judging from the sun shining that day, Toronto was clearly favoured by the elements. The streets were full of pedestrians out for fresh air, despite the heat. As we drove across the city, I had a feeling of freedom beyond anything I'd ever known. It was a state of mind devoid of any fear, any vulnerability. I was giddy with the power of the car and felt invincible in that futuristic-looking machine. Maria loved speed and drove in the fast lane, negotiating turns with some timely braking. Everything around us became ephemeral. Skyscrapers, stores, and passersby all disappeared in the blink of an eye. The speed of the red racer was literally intoxicating. Maria was taking me along in her four-wheeled rocket. She gave me the impression that she was granting me a privilege, that she trusted me. Because if you had to risk your life with someone, you wouldn't do it with just anyone. In any event, she was with the right person: I liked speed. In sharing these fearless moments, we were becoming friends. I was making my first friend in Toronto, the first white friend in my life. Maria turned onto Bloor Street West and headed toward Ossington. We drove past multicoloured streamers, which were in reality the summer clothes of the people on the sidewalks. The traffic lights changed to the rhythm of the Counting Crows playing on the radio, the drums as precise and steady as Swiss clockwork. At that moment, Toronto morphed into one huge rock concert. Then, the CN Tower, one of the seven wonders of the modern world, rose up, flashing and cloud-free. My euphoria grew upon seeing that mile-high structure, its spire pointing heavenward and dominating the city admirably. As I continued to gaze at it, I began to feel dizzy. Yet, in this fast-moving car, we were already feeling another type of dizziness, another type of elation. The life flowing through our veins was coursing beyond the arteries of the city.

"Is the country you're from very far from Mozambique?" asked

Maria, pulling me from my sensations.

"Yes," I replied, roused from my experience.

The light at which we'd stopped turned green. The wheels of the Corvette screeched again, and we outdistanced the cars behind us.

"My father lived in Mozambique," she said, looking in her rear-view. "But that was before he met my mother. Are people fighting where you come from, too?"

"No."

Then I thought of Bijou and added, "It's every man for himself."

"Pardon?"

"Nothing."

I went back to looking at the streamers on the sidewalks. South of Ossington, Maria slowed down and came to a stop in front of a house with a red synthetic-tile roof. It looked very similar to the others in the neighbourhood. There were pots of flowers in the windows. On the gate, an image of Christ on the cross. We entered a small garden with a fountain of cherubs sprinkling a perfectly manicured lawn. There was nothing luxurious about the place, but the care taken made it look quaint. An old burgundy couch sat on the veranda.

Maria opened the front door, saying, "After you, Raymond. It's too late to change your mind now."

She laughed and gestured that there was nothing to fear. Even so, as I entered the house, I wondered how her parents would react when they saw me.

"Remember," she whispered, "you're a friend from school. Okay?"

I nodded.

After walking down a narrow hallway with a polished wood floor, we entered the living room. A greying man wearing shabby green slippers was sitting in front of the television. He made a pretence of greeting us, without really exerting himself. He had thinning hair and slumped shoulders. His plaid shirt and black pants revealed a certain corpulence, sagging with the years. The curtains were drawn so that the room stood in semidarkness, only the television emitting beams of light and a lamp with a yellowish shade casting a dim glow. Maria introduced me to her father, Fernando Da Costa. He gave me a quick smile, to get it over with as soon as possible and continue watching his Portuguese program. Then he motioned me to sit down in an armchair. Maria tried to say something to him in Portuguese, but the volume of the TV drowned out her voice.

The living room furniture, large and drab, rested on a thick white wool rug. Photographs of weddings, baptisms, and communions covered the walls. Amid these images of family memories hung a picture of Christ in Mary's arms, the two recognizable by their spiritual fullness and the halos around their heads. Fernando was drinking something that looked like cognac. He went and fetched a glass from the cabinet and set it down on the coffee table.

"Port?"

I found his offer early, given the time of day. Seeing my hesitation, he insisted,

"Yes, yes, port!"

He poured a red liquid over ice cubes in a stemless glass. We drank a sip or two in silence.

"Ah!" he said, eyeing his drink appreciatively. "Where you from?"

"Benin."

"Oh, I was in Mozambique," he announced proudly.

He clasped his hands around his glass. Without waiting for me to answer, he continued, "Yes, yes, I knew Mozambique before it became independent." A glimmer of nostalgia appeared in his eyes.

Maria had gone to her room, and Fernando went back to watching his program. I drank my port in silence. Thick and burning, it went slowly down my throat and directly into my bloodstream. Heat rose up in me like magma erupting in a forgotten volcano. The room seemed more and more stifling, and a torrid cocoon was gradually forming around me. Fernando offered me another glass. I politely declined, but he insisted again,

"A last little one! For the road."

His imperfect English was understandable enough. He raised his glass to a Portuguese soccer club.

"And to national team in Cameroon!" he said, smiling. "That's where you're from, isn't it?"

"Um . . . Yes," I said, to keep it simple.

In putting my glass down on the coffee table, I noticed a large map of Portugal under the see-through top. On it appeared the words, "I love Portugal."

"Nice map you have here . . ."

"Ah! yes, beautiful country. I'd still be there if the leftists hadn't gotten in."

We fell silent again. The television program ended and a soccer game began. This time, Fernando forgot that I existed.

Maria reappeared, which suited me just fine.

"You're lucky my mother's not here," she whispered in my ear.

Then, seeing my puzzled expression, she added, laughing, "I'm kidding . . . she's very charming."

Maria was ready to go. Fernando was even more distant in bidding us goodbye than he was in greeting us. We left the house, Maria walking out first. She had changed into a light, loose-fitting blue dress that fluttered in the slightest gust of air. In the car, she removed her sunglasses and fixed her hair in the rear-view. I went through her music collection while she was touching up her eyeliner.

"So? What did you think of my father?" she asked, raising an eyebrow.

"He's nice."

"No, honestly, what did you think of him?"

"He's nice," I repeated, looking her in the eye.

"You're not telling me the truth. I'll take your answer for now. But the next time I ask you . . . I want the truth."

Her face became expressionless. She held my gaze for a few more seconds to make sure that I'd taken her seriously. Her comment seemed like a threat. I thought the whole thing was ridiculous. I couldn't see myself telling her that her father smelled like port from a distance, that he needed a good shower and, above all, to go into detox. Fernando was in pathetic shape. Admitting that to his daughter would've been cruel. I didn't want to hurt her.

Maria drove, holding the steering wheel firmly with both hands. I took the opportunity to admire her rings. On her one hand, a silver snake was wrapped around her thumb beside an all-blue eye. On her other hand, an open-mouthed skull sparkled next to a Star of David. Maria's taste seemed to be more original than elegant.

Given the speed at which we were moving, the streamers started to reappear on the sidewalks. The Corvette, Maria, and I had once again become elusive. After a few moments of silence, she asked me again,

"So, what did you think of the old man?"

"I think he's a nice man! I already told you that."

Maria swore in Portuguese.

"Who do you think I am? Your mother? Oh, you're lying to me because we made love. Is that it? Men! I hate your crappy sentimentalism! Just because a woman gives herself to you, you start acting stupid and uptight. You don't dare tell it like it is. You listen to me, Raymond. Stop getting all soft when I ask you for the truth. Stop feeling like you have to lie. If anyone should be sentimental right now, it's me. Because if I dump you here in the middle of the city, you surely don't have a cent to get back to that sardine can you live in at Jane and Finch. Let me tell you something. If you don't want to have to lie your whole life, stop being sentimental, okay? Say what you think."

I didn't reply. Maria had reduced me to silence. She'd easily found what it took to upset me. I was starting to be afraid of her and her fits of anger, which overwhelmed me. I was terrified at the thought of being stuck in the city if she decided to leave me in the lurch. I was completely thrown by my powerlessness. Even if I didn't have a cent, there was no point in reminding me of it, except to hurt me. My temples were burning with pain. I kept quiet for quite some time so it would pass. I was a weight, as heavy as an anvil. I was a burden in the Corvette. I should've never come with her. But I couldn't have hung around the apartment by myself, staring at the ceiling, looking like a fool.

Maria drove in silence. She glanced over at me from time to time to see if she could make out what I was thinking. I was mulling over the last thing she'd said, "Say what you think." It wasn't easy. But, if I had to, I'd start with her, the person I hated the most at that moment. She'd hurt me on purpose.

"I'm sorry, I didn't mean to offend you," she said in a very soft voice.

I didn't respond. An ambulance, all lights flashing, flew right by our car, which had stopped. The sirens were spitting red and white venom. The incident was alarming, disorienting. In the blink of an eye, Toronto had taken on a different face, had become startling and indomitable. The stupefying sounds of car engines starting back up made my head spin. In the distance, I heard a voice asking me if I was still angry. It was Toronto's voice, both warm and rough. Maria's voice.

"You're not saying anything. You're not going to sulk for long, are you?"

"No. Let's not talk about it anymore," I said curtly.

"You know, I didn't mean to . . ."

"Don't you go getting sentimental. It's not like you."

"That's true."

"I think your father drinks too much. Is he homesick?"

"A little, but there's something else. It's hard to understand. He started overdoing it when he lost his job at Public Works. Maybe he was just waiting for an excuse to get drunk," suggested the psychology student. "Sometimes I judge him too harshly because I'm his daughter. Other times, I don't judge him at all. It's true that he talks about going back to Portugal . . . but he's been talking about it for such a long time. He left Portugal for a new life. But when he got here, he never changed anything. The only thing that was different was his job. Now that he doesn't have that, he's bored, he complains, he feels sorry for himself. I hope you won't become like that."

I didn't say a word. I didn't have the answer.

A Summer's Day on Lake Shore Boulevard

The Corvette turned onto Lake Shore Boulevard. The street was full of tourists swarming around all sorts of vendors, like bees around a hive. We drove past beautiful pleasure boats by the shore of a shimmering lake. Latin American musicians were strumming their guitars. The smell of hot dogs and French fries hung in the air. Maria parked near the water's edge, not far from a sumptuous building, and we walked to the entrance without a word. The magical echo of Indian flutes reached my ears and captivated me. I felt like joining the tourists, who were soaking up the sun and relishing life. The atmosphere was jovial, but what I liked best was the heterogeneous nature of the scene. The most diverse folks had come out and were mixing on a summer's afternoon. For the occasion, the different communities seemed to have overcome their fear of the others. In looking at these people, I imagined a modern painting, a collage. I pictured Toronto as a work of art in which various colours coexisted. I saw an image of hot dogs, hungry gulls, and sombreros in dazzling kitsch.

Maria and I took a gleaming elevator in the cool lobby. She drew two letters out of her purse and slipped them into her bodice. On exiting, we started down a clean, polished, silent hallway. The tourists outside, the Latinos and their music, already belonged to another world. The lighting here was subdued and the air almost cold, with hints of chic perfume lingering here and there. Maria wore her blue dress with elegance, her spike heels resounding in the corridor. I was walking behind her, gazing at her dark hair, which shone from time to time as her silver earrings jingled. All the apartment doors were black. Maria rang the bell at one of them. Although the sound was inaudible to us, the door opened almost immediately. A young woman with green eyes smiled at Maria, and they kissed each other cheerfully. Behind her stood another woman who was older and wearing more makeup; her mother, I thought.

"Do come in," said the older woman in a formal tone. "We were about to have a cup of tea."

Maria introduced us, but couldn't remember exactly what country I was from. To tease her, I said I was from Mozambique. She frowned slightly, making it clear that she knew I wasn't from there. I smiled at her, amused. We were invited into the apartment, which was luxurious. The floor was so clean that you could see yourself in it. Even the rugs seemed to shine with cleanliness. Most of the furniture was made of wood, some pieces combining wood with glass or wrought iron. Surrealist paintings hung on the white walls. Hardcover books and women's magazines were lined up on the shelves. A few pastel candles, and many multicoloured shells in transparent vases, added touches of lightness. In the dining room, two candelabras adorned either side of a black buffet. A porcelain tea service sat in the centre. That was the one we used.

The four of us settled into the living room. The two women bombarded Maria with questions about what she'd been doing. While they did so, I looked out the picture window in front of me, admiring Lake Ontario, which was glistening for miles around.

Maria and her lovely green-eyed friend decided to retire so they could talk more privately. I found myself alone with the lady who had offered us tea. She had refined manners, almost precious. She drank her tea with her little finger raised.

Mrs Philips had fine lines at the corners of her eyes and lips. She wore magnificent jewelry on her coarse-skinned hands, including a ring with a huge blue stone that turned greenish every time she lifted her cup. A subtle fragrance emanated from her clothing. Her lace blouse had sharp fold creases and her light brown skirt knife-edge pleats. Fine white silk stockings covered her slender bony legs and led to flat-heeled shoes.

Comfortably seated, Mrs Philips started to tell me about her flowers, which she was trying to keep from wilting in this infernal summer heat. There were certainly flowers on her terrace, quivering in the breeze. As I listened to her, I savoured these moments in her company. Not because of her undeniable charm, but because of the light conversation about her flowers. It was impossible for me to see myself sitting in her living room in Cotonou. I would've had to be her gardener for her to be talking to me about flowers there. I wanted to tell her that I'd never talked about roses the way she did, with passion and concern. In fact, I'd never talked about roses, period. To me, her beloved roses were an enigma, like classical music. I didn't know anything about roses. I'd only seen them in the gardens of Europeans in Benin. I refrained from telling her so, since she might not have appreciated it. After all, our conversation was pleasant. Mrs Philips wondered why such fragile flowers had been created. It was sad, she thought, to see them wilt so quickly.

"I don't think flowers are fragile. In my opinion, they're very hardy."

"What do you mean?"

"Well, I don't think anyone could spend months underground with all those germs and vermin, then come up blossoming like a flower."

"You know, I hadn't thought of it that way. You're very poetic. In any event, from the way you see it, flowers are certainly hardier than me."

She vigorously stirred her tea, which was getting cold.

"What do you plan to do now that you're in Canada?"

"What do you mean?" I asked, to buy time. I had no idea. All I knew for sure was that I'd be starting from scratch. Again, I refrained from telling her the truth, that I didn't have a plan. I didn't want to seem irresponsible. I was going to lie. I had to say something. But what?

"You're very witty, you're smart, you're young. What do you want to do?"

"Well . . . to be honest, I don't know."

She set down her cup, looking surprised.

"You don't know?"

"Well, let's say that I have a vague idea . . . I'd like to spend my days visiting charming ladies and discussing roses, cats, and fragrances with great conviction."

Mrs Philips turned pale with embarrassment, then disguised her lack of composure with a fitting smile.

"Are you saying that I'm not a good conversationalist, young man?"

"No, not at all. On the contrary. I'd like to be able to talk about new things here in Canada. I want to start a new life and I think the best way to do that is to stop having the same topics of conversation. Do you know what I mean?"

"Oh, yes! I suppose that a young man never takes care of planting roses . . . only picking them."

"Now you're the one who's being witty," I said in an amused tone. "I mean it, though. To talk about flowers the way you do, you have to love them . . . or be rich. I'd like to learn how to love flowers . . . or become rich."

"Perhaps that's the way to go . . . but you'll find that what everyone here wants is to stay young. To have eternal youth."

"Why youth?"

Mrs Philips smiled.

"Because no one can buy youth. Not even me," she said smiling again, this time ironically.

"You don't need to buy it."

Elizabeth seemed flustered. My eyes lingered on her lace blouse. She noticed my gaze.

"One could say that you're bold."

She set down her cup slowly, her eyes lowered. I seized the opportunity to lay my hand on hers. She quickly pulled her hand away.

Marie returned with her friend. We had to leave. Both mother and daughter accompanied us to the elevator.

"It was a pleasure," said Elizabeth, her eyes meeting mine.

Maria promised to come back very soon.

Maria and the Philips Family

In the car, Maria was keen on telling me about the Philips family. The lady with whom I'd been speaking was Elizabeth Philips, the wife of Derek Philips, a pulp and paper baron and the president of a very prosperous company in Vancouver. Elizabeth was in Toronto to help her daughter, who was recovering from a breakdown. Ann Philips, the beautiful green-eyed girl, had fallen in love with a Chinese man from Hong Kong named David Lee. The fellow was a kingpin in the Chinese underworld plaguing the West Coast of Canada. Officially, he had made his fortune in real estate. If you were to combine his assets with those of his cousins, you could say that Vancouver belonged to his family. David was twice divorced and considerably older than Ann. They'd met at a select sports club and instantly fallen for each other. Because of their affair, which scandalized Vancouver's upper crust, Derek Philips had decided to send his only child to Toronto. Once Ann was isolated here, she suffered a breakdown and even contemplated suicide. One night she called her father and told him that she was going to throw herself out the window. Derek managed to talk her out of it. Since that incident, a private detective had been following her everywhere and watching her as carefully as possible.

Elizabeth didn't dare tell Ann that she was opposed to the relationship, because she wasn't close to her. She never had been. She deeply regretted that she'd never been able to talk to Ann like a mother, to express her affection. Sometimes, she wondered if she was even capable of having such warm feelings for her daughter. She'd run off on her all the time, going from one women's convention to another. She'd slipped out to scholarly women's cocktail receptions. She'd done the rounds of charitable organizations, even though they were full of gossips and greedy people. Her response to Ann's crisis—a final, awkward attempt meant to be loving—was to jump on a plane to join her daughter. Now that she was here in Toronto, she wondered if she'd come more for Derek's sake. After all, he'd made love to her the night before she left, as if to convince her to go. Maybe deep down, she wanted more drama in her life, to increase those moments of intimacy with Derek which had become so rare.

"How do you know all that? How do you know that he made love to her?" I asked.

"Because I know everything!" she replied, with an impish little smile.

"Were you in their bed in Vancouver?"

"In a way," she said enigmatically.

Maria waited for my reaction. She wanted me to go on asking questions more eagerly. She wanted to see me rocking in my seat and stamping my feet with impatience, anxious to understand. I didn't want to give her the satisfaction. So I remained silent. I wasn't interested in playing her game.

We were driving west on Bloor, a street that runs across the city like a golden band. The gods, drunk with their power, seemed to have scattered skyscrapers here and there on Bloor, like towers of Babel, from which businessmen in sober suits—a briefcase in one hand and a cell phone in the other—were emerging. Further along, fruits and vegetables were displayed in front of grocers, their colours rivalling those of the traffic lights. I'd never seen vegetables so green or apples and oranges so fresh and bright in my entire life. I was hardly able to contain my bewilderment as I gazed, astounded, at these fruits of the earth dazzling the sidewalks with their purity and perfection. Never at the Dantokpa Market in Cotonou—that oven where vendors were dying of heat—had I seen such healthy produce. I was uncomfortable with these sights because I realized how unfamiliar I was with the beauty of fruit, with the beauty of things.

Maria's eyes were hidden behind her sunglasses. She pointed to a building.

"That's where I take my psych classes. We're going through the University of Toronto campus."

Cyclists were riding between the administrative buildings. Those Victorian structures were surrounded by snack bars and pizza parlors, packed with hungry students. This was the first time I'd passed through a campus without seeing even a single soldier.

Bloor Street was bursting with vitality. At every intersection, its appearance changed. It morphed and found new energy, new effervescence.

Maria's Revelation

Maria could no longer bear the silence I was inflicting on her, silence that she took for indifference.

"Okay. I know everything about the Philips family because I'm having an affair with Derek."

"Pardon?"

"You heard me."

"Does your good friend, Ann, know about this?"

"Of course not!" she said, irritated. "I wouldn't ruin a friendship over an affair."

"You're not being honest, Maria," I said very bluntly, to conceal my anger. "You want me to tell the truth, but you're not being honest yourself."

"Well, I have a feeling I won't be the only one playing this game for much longer. I saw you squirming with pleasure, talking to Elizabeth. You were in seventh heaven. The woman had you eating out of her hand. If she had've told you to unzip your pants, you would've done it. You were just waiting for it. So don't come and tell me that I'm being dishonest. You could be in the same situation very soon. Okay?"

"Why are you friends with your lover's wife and daughter?"

"Because I'm interested in the melodramatic lives of the rich. Because I'd like to make my way into the upper class. Because I'm ambitious. Are those reasons enough for you?"

"Enough for me to know what to think of you."

"Oh, don't be so self-righteous, Raymond. It doesn't suit you. You know very well that what motivates me could motivate you, too. After all, Mrs Philips thought you were very nice."

Elizabeth's face came to mind. It looked like one of those slightly creased, white pages forgotten in the back of a desk. A face with fine lines certain of their path. In her presence, I didn't remember feeling poorer or blacker than her, or less able to make my way. I admitted to myself that I didn't dislike the idea of getting involved with her. I quickly dismissed the thought and was sorry I'd ever had it. I turned to Maria and told her that I didn't want to talk about the Philips family anymore. We drove on in silence for several moments, silence that was heavy and forced.

The Corvette turned onto Jane and headed north. The houses lining the street had identical staircases leading up to the front stoops. The windows, too, all looked alike. The impressive buildings had disappeared. We were passing a growing number of modest families walking home from doing their shopping. Despite the late afternoon sun, a sort of greyness stole over the sky, covering the area with a bleak light.

Maria was the one who broke the silence.

"Listen, I'm no angel. But God knows that I don't wish anyone any harm," she said, making the sign of the cross, "not Elizabeth, anyway. I'll tell you how I met her husband."

"No thank you," I replied promptly, almost without thinking.

"Why? Are you afraid?"

"Me? Afraid of what?"

I was in fact afraid to hear what she had to say. The thought of having an affair with Elizabeth might cross my mind again. I didn't want to admit that I would've liked to do the same thing as Maria.

"Listen to me. I insist."

I shook my head.

"Well, you don't have a choice. I met Derek at the Royal York Hotel, in the heart of the business district. I was going to a conference on industrial psychology there. I went to the wrong room and ended up at a conference on deforestation. I was so well dressed that I was mistaken for a speaker and seated next to him. When I realized what had happened, he asked me to stay. By then, it was too late for me to refuse him anything. I no longer had the will to leave. Do you know what I mean?"

"No," I replied curtly.

"Yes, you do. You know what I mean. Just back there, you couldn't pull yourself away from Elizabeth. It was the same for me with Derek. Even before he spoke to me, I knew I couldn't resist him. Rich people don't need to charm poor people. All they have to do is be polite to them. You know . . . I don't regret anything. Derek is no Prince Charming, but he's a nice guy."

Maria stroked the dashboard with the back of her hand.

"And Ann? How did you meet her?" I asked, slightly embarrassed by my curiosity.

"I met her later on. Derek really loves her. A friend of his introduced us when she got to Toronto. Ann and I have something in common."

"What's that?"

"Parents who don't love each other anymore and who are tearing each other apart."

An Unexpected Stop

M aria decided to stop at a fish market in the suburbs to make a last-minute purchase. We walked into the store, and she called out to a teenager who was putting packages away in the freezer. He turned around and recognized Maria, a broad smile appearing on his lips. He came over to her, speaking Portuguese, his brown hair falling in his eyes. His short, plump physique still had something childlike about it.

"He sings in the choir every Sunday," explained Maria.

She kissed him on the cheek. He smiled at her, then quickly disappeared behind a door hidden in the back.

"Did you see that? He blushed! Oh, if I was fifteen, I wouldn't let that one get away."

"One day, you'll have to tell me why you love men so much. And even those who aren't men yet," I said, to provoke her.

"It's not men I love, it's life. And men are a part of it . . . When I was young, I used to hear my parents making love in their bedroom next to mine. They were happy in those days. They don't love each other anymore, they just put up with each other. I don't want that to happen to me. I want to have as much love as possible so that I never run short."

A man in his forties with a bushy mustache made his way toward us. He looked like the owner of the store. Maria seemed to know him well. He was short, with a potbelly and broad shoulders. He started rummaging through the freezer. Maria turned to me.

"My mother may have been faithful, but that didn't stop her from being unhappy. Besides . . . what do you know about my secret desires?" she asked, a touch of mischief in her eyes. "Can you guess what my fantasies are? Hmmm? Maybe I like them in their teens."

"You mean boys?"

"I didn't say just boys!"

I opened my eyes wide in surprise. Maria choked back her laughter.

"Okay, I don't know anything about your fantasies," I admitted, "but I'd like to."

Maria didn't reply. She squinted slightly as if trying to read something too far away. Then she turned around and took the bag the owner was holding out to her. I caught a glimpse of a frozen octopus.

"It's for my father. When my mother cooks it for him, he's not nearly as homesick."

As we walked back to the car, Maria was swaying her hips more than when we went into the store. I bit my lip, my desire flaring up like a bushfire. I thought about her fantasies again. Did she want me to take her right here, in front of stunned Torontonians? Devour her in front of highly excited voyeurs? That was, in fact, one of my repressed desires. I wondered if people on every continent had the same fantasies. I didn't know about the hidden desires of the men and women in my country. It was taboo to talk about them. My thoughts had distracted me slightly from Maria's hips, but my eyes returned to her silhouette. She was nearing the car, holding the bag with a limp hand, her chest straight and her lips slightly parted. I wanted to have my way with her on the hood of the Corvette. I laid my hand gently on her shoulder. She immediately moved away.

"The more I look at you, the less I understand what you want. You're so changeable."

She frowned while settling into the car, then drove in silence. Eventually she decided to speak.

"Are there transvestites where you come from?"

"No."

"Do you celebrate Gay Pride?"

"Gay what?"

She burst out laughing.

"There's no reason to be shocked. And no, I'm not a lesbian in case you were wondering. Although I have tried same sex. Have you?"

"No. And I'm not shocked. I'm just surprised, that's all."

"Raymond, I'm still trying to figure out who I am. I'm entitled to do that. Everyone here is trying to figure out who they are. If the people where you come from are happy with the missionary position, well, good for them!"

"That's not what I mean," I said. "What I'm criticizing is that you claim to be pious when, in fact, you're no more pious than me."

Maria put on some Cuban music. That was her way of saying that the discussion was over. I wasn't so concerned about the dangerous game she was playing as I was about my own behaviour. Was I really more honest than her? How many times had I sunk into a woman knowing that I was only after my own pleasure? I waited until night to be the man I wasn't during the day. Maria had many lives, like a cat. Who was I to criticize her for her ambiguity? I was trying to be different, to be better, but I wasn't convinced that I was succeeding. Maria was well aware of that.

We weren't very far from Finch Avenue. Maria seemed more relaxed after telling me all that. She lit a cigarette as she drove along.

"Maria, I want you to know that I don't have any intention of pursuing Elizabeth."

"That's good."

"Why? Are you jealous?" I asked, laughing.

"Oh, come on, don't be silly. No, it's good for you, because Elizabeth's been feeling fragile lately. She's usually faithful, but she might be capable of doing anything to forget her troubles."

Maria had just rekindled my temptation. She added, maybe to ease her conscience, that she took mail to Ann Philips, love letters from David Lee.

"When you betray someone, you'd better comfort them as well. That way, when you're held accountable before God, you won't be completely guilty."

She kissed the cross on her necklace and slipped it back in her bodice.

The Corvette stopped in front of my building. As I climbed out of the car, I asked,

"Why did you tell me all that, Maria?"

She removed her sunglasses and smiled sadly.

"It's not easy to explain."

"Try. You know, I admit that everything you said about me . . . and Mrs Philips has some truth to it. But one thing's for sure, I'm not like you yet."

"I disgust you, don't I?"

"No, not at all. I like you. And if you confided in me, it's because you like me too. Right?"

"No, that's not why. I confided in you because I don't regret anything I do. What's more, I don't care if you see Elizabeth again."

Maria put her sunglasses back on.

"It's about this morning. I don't want you to take me for some little fling to tell your buddies about. I don't want you to say to them, "Oh, I screwed a goddamn white girl the other day."

"But . . ."

"Let me finish. You know a lot about me now. You've met my father. You've even met the person I'm betraying. Maybe I'm a slut in your eyes or a hypocrite. But I'm someone now. I'm not just the object of your desire anymore. I'm Maria and I exist. Do you understand?"

"I think so."

I closed the car door, still stunned by what she'd said. She took off like a shot, honked from a distance, and disappeared into the traffic. I felt abandoned. Maria had already become an elusive whirlwind again on the streets of Toronto.

Returning to the Fold

There were only a few people on their balconies at that time. It would soon be getting dark. Those who were still out didn't react when they saw me. I entered the building, strode down the dimly lit hallway and stepped onto the elevator. A great commotion could be heard on every floor. People were darting off the elevator at the last moment. Children were entertaining themselves by pressing the button on every level.

When I entered the apartment, Bob and Joseph were playing cards. Koffi hadn't come home yet. A tropical cyclone of Caribbean music was swirling through the living room. The tones and beats of congas, trumpets, and percussions were surging around the players. Bob's dreadlocks were hanging in his face. He was eyeing his opponent between his ringlets, wearing a secretive smile. Joseph was knitting his brow in concentration. Despite his squinting, he couldn't help humming the tune.

All of a sudden, the sound of trumpets burst forth and unfurled like a furious, raging wave.

"Ah, now that's music!" declared Joseph, his gaze suddenly far from the game.

Bob shook his head with a mocking look.

"Who's that singing?" I asked.

"An old Haitian," replied Joseph. "They're the ones who still know how to sing. The stuff people are putting out today is useless. They all want to imitate each other."

Joseph had barely finished speaking when he jumped up and leapt around the room.

"I beat you! I beat you! Didn't I?"

"Yeah, you won," admitted Bob.

Joseph held out his hand.

"Cough up the dough, man! You owe me twenty bucks."

Bob made good on his bet. Joseph planted a kiss on the bill.

"Why don't we order a pizza?"

Joseph asked Bob to call for one. While Bob was doing so, Joseph took me aside to question me.

"So, how's Maria?"

"She's fine. She's a nice girl."

"You see, you're living with people who have good taste."

"Yes, Joseph. You have very good taste."

I wasn't sure what he meant by that. Joseph understood that if he wanted more information about my afternoon with Maria, he'd have to worm it out of me.

"You're not very talkative, are you?"

"What do you want me to tell you? She showed me around town, took me to see some friends of hers . . . and brought me back here."

"Didn't she give you a message for me?"

"Yes," I fibbed, to shut him up. "She told me to say hello for her."

Joseph didn't push the matter any further. We listened to the music while waiting for the pizza.

The Club

Koffi got home much earlier than usual. We were all in the living room watching television. An old movie about the Second World War had managed to capture our attention. Koffi greeted us quickly and got straight into the shower. When he returned to the living room, he announced, "Brothers, I'm going to work at a nightclub not very far from here . . . You feel like coming?"

"Yeah," said Bob, getting to his feet almost immediately.

"Let's go," added Joseph.

On the way downstairs, Joseph explained that the bar where Koffi worked was an after-hours and that he sometimes went there when Koffi invited him.

"It's a very interesting place," he said, without elaborating. He seemed to be keeping something secret.

Outside, a fine rain had fallen. The wet concrete shone under the streetlights, and small puddles glimmered here and there. Our shadows—those of four young men—grew enormously on the pavement, then quickly disappeared as if they'd seen the devil himself. Our footfalls resounded in the late-night air. And our pure, almost spontaneous laughter protected us from the vast darkness.

I remember that outing because it was the first evening I'd spent in the company of all my roommates. We'd left the drab walls that served as our home and felt invigorated. The conversation seemed to come more easily. Bob had tied his hair back at his nape, and I could admire his large sparkling eyes. He was gesturing in the dark, waving his arms like a conjurer. He was talking to Koffi about music, explaining how he'd managed to learn a pattern of notes on his guitar. He was visibly delighted. He had just conquered a new segment of a world he intended to master. Koffi listened quietly, then asked the musician to advise him on what to play at the club. Bob remained silent for a few moments, staring up at the black, star-speckled sky. The night was a cathedral—a cathedral with the most pearl-adorned vault on earth. Bob gave his advice in a knowledgeable but unpretentious manner, with passion in his eyes. He knew how to convince, like a priest in his church, like a guru before his followers.

The cars made a ripping sound as they flew by on the wet pavement. With their piercing headlights, they looked like meteorites returning to a dark point in the universe.

Joseph also seemed happy to be out. He'd turned up his collar because of the slight chill in the air. You could still see a sort of relief on the side of his face. He was walking without a word—the man who usually talked all the time.

Bob and Joseph appeared to me in a new light. The street lamps revealed two sensitive souls capable of being moved. They had more in them than just anger, after all.

Toronto by Night

Koffi's job was in the basement of a bland house on a lane with a pretentious name: York Gate Boulevard. Outside, there wasn't a soul around. Everything was quiet. Koffi rang the bell three times slowly, then twice more quickly. The door opened, and a young girl with a rather sullen expression showed us in. She directed us to the basement, and Koffi invited us to follow him down. There was complete silence in the entrance, not a single note of music reaching my ears. As we descended the staircase, we started to hear a song, which was muted at first, then grew louder and louder. The steps led down to a smoke-filled room the size of a postage stamp. The place was furnished with a few rickety round tables, each surrounded by four or five chairs. Some people were gesticulating on a tiny dance floor, circled overhead by cheap multicoloured lights. Other guests, slumped in their chairs, were dozing in the din. An aging woman behind a mock bamboo bar was serving drinks almost mechanically, without a hint of a smile.

I was surprised by Koffi's nightclub. What amazed me most was that none of this racket could be heard outside. Why did all these souls need to go underground, to sink into the bowels of the earth, when life awaited them above. There were some forty people in the basement— all black except one white man—bent on enjoying themselves to the point of passing out. They were writhing around like fish out of water, with the determination that only fish show before they die. The dancers, for their part, wanted nothing more than to drown themselves in the pleasures and delights of reeling bodies, covered in the salt of their own sweat.

The strong smell of smoke caught in my throat and made my head spin.

"Are you okay?" asked Koffi.

"Yes, just a little dizzy."

Koffi took me by the arm, and we crossed the room to the bar.

"Some good Jamaican rum'll perk you up," he said after ordering. "You weren't expecting this, were you?" he added, pointing to the people on the dance floor.

"No . . . Not at all."

"That's how it is here, Brother! There's what you see and what you don't."

Koffi slipped away to relieve the DJ, who was waiting for him in the booth. Bob and Joseph had dispersed and were chatting with people they seemed to know well.

The DJ that Koffi was replacing wasn't a young man. He was the owner of the club and had decided to earn some extra money by turning his basement into an illegal nightclub. He'd posted his daughter at the front door. His wife was in charge of the bar and the cash, and his son had the task of throwing out the undesirables. He operated the control booth. Since he was getting on in years, he had Koffi take over for him some nights.

The mother, plump and phenomenally buxom, came over to us holding three beers. She handed me one and left immediately. Weaving her way admirably through the crowd, she skirted slender, thickset and transparently-clad figures before ending up back behind the bar. I watched her, my beer in my hand and my eyes already yellow from the rum I'd just gulped. Her gait reminded me of a bomb-disposal expert zigzagging through a minefield. And she was right to be cautious. This small place, smelling of smoke, sweat and beer, was above all a battlefield. Every overheated dancer was an explosive to be handled with care. The level of energy in the room could've set the entire house ablaze. What's more, no one in this underground world had any regard for anyone else. We were in a realm that wasn't part of ordinary life. No one had the right to lay down the law. The devil could've been any one of us, and he was not to be provoked.

The cheapness of the decor reminded me of certain places in Cotonou. The tacky ornaments hanging here and there created the offbeat atmosphere of clubs where people celebrate to forget that they don't have money. The dull, distasteful lights were no longer flashing much. The air was growing thicker with smoke. I thought I was going to have another dizzy spell, but the beer took care of reviving me. The lights continued to dim, succumbing to jaundice, scarlet fever, and every other disease on the face of the earth.

A dance train came out of nowhere and snatched me up before I could do anything about it. Male dancers in an orgiastic mood were holding the hips of callipygian women. I was behind a man who was so drunk he was having trouble keeping step. I was holding up the rest of the train because he reeked so badly of rum that I didn't want to get too close to him. Strong hands suddenly grabbed hold of my shoulders. Hot, nauseating breath said in my ear, "Hey, Koffi just told me about you, Brother! Follow me."

I turned around and saw only a greying, black nape. The man sat down at a table with a beaming, gold-toothed woman. He pulled up a chair and insisted that I join him. His bloodshot eyes softened when I complied.

"Koffi told me that you're from Benin. Is that true?"

"Yes."

"Then you're a brother! I'm from Upper Volta!"

"Upper Volta? You mean Burkina Faso."

"Oh, yeah! I always forget that my country changed its name. You know, I've been here for such a long time."

He roared with laughter at the mistake and relayed the incident to the obese woman, who showed all of the jewellery in her mouth.

"I'm Mathieu Zongo," he said, shaking my hand with an iron grip. "And you are?"

"Raymond," I replied, grimacing with pain, my hand being clenched.

"So, tell me! How are things in Africa?" he asked, his breath fouler than ever. His baritone voice was thick with whiskey. I pictured myself at the end of the evening with the same red eyes. He laid his hand on his girlfriend's thigh and whispered something in her ear. She laughed, gave me a sidelong glance, lifted all her weight, and disappeared into the crowd that was dancing more and more outside the dance floor.

"You like her?"

"She's not my type."

"Be careful, Brother," he cautioned, chuckling. "Don't be foolish enough to take a woman from here!"

"Why do you think I'd do that?"

"I don't know," he replied, gulping his drink. "I don't have much faith in the young people I've seen landing here in the past few years. I wonder how you were all raised . . ."

Mathieu looked at me, a burning question in his eyes.

"What is it?" I asked.

"Well, you can't even talk to me about Africa. That's not normal!"

Mathieu emptied his glass, and his girlfriend returned with another drink. He thanked her with a slap on the hip.

"In my day," he continued, "I would've jumped for joy to meet a big African brother just a few days after I arrived. You don't seem to give a hoot!"

"Do you have a job for me?" I asked bluntly.

"No, I'm looking for one myself."

"Do you have a place to share?"

"No," repeated Mathieu. I could see the surprise in his eyes. That's what I wanted. I didn't like his brotherly tone.

"Koffi, on the other hand, gave me his bed. How do I know that you're my brother? Because you're African and you bought me a drink?"

The mixture of rum and beer was having a very bad effect on my mind. Mathieu's fiery eyes widened. His amazement gave way to anger.

"Well, I'll be damned! Africa's really in a bad way. You listen to me, boy," he said in a threatening tone. "I'm going to tell you a story that's very short but important. There was once a man who was young like you. He fought for his country's independence. When hatred and corruption were ravaging his homeland, he risked his life to denounce them. Then he had to go into exile to save his hide and keep his integrity in the eyes of his kids. Today, he's sitting in a bar, far away from his family, with a young man who's not showing him any respect. And he wonders if he would've have been better off becoming corrupt."

We remained silent, looking at each other in that basement unknown to the outside world. His eyes rolled upward, shot through with blades of light, blazing with rage. When the blazing disappeared, I sensed that he was about to deflagrate inwardly, in a silent tumult on the verge of tears. That didn't affect my insolence or my tone. I shouted that if young people like me didn't respect him, it was because there weren't any more young people in Africa, only desperate ones. It wasn't a question of a prosperous future, but of survival.

I had offended a stranger who never would've spoken to me had he known what awaited him. He wasn't the real cause of my anger. I'd spit venom for one reason. I wanted to part ways with the brotherhood of the oppressed, the very one in which I'd grown up. My anger was directed at a relentless enemy: imperialism. All Africans learned to stand in solidarity with the oppressed before they learned to read. With this man, it was the same old story. But I was in Toronto to turn the page. And no one, not even an unsung hero, was going to stop me. No one was going to shatter my dream.

Mathieu clenched his fists. I took this gesture as a final warning before he exploded. The little sobriety I had left enabled me to move away. I returned to the bar where another beer that Koffi had ordered was waiting for me.

Maybe Mathieu was telling the truth. Maybe he couldn't be corrupted. It was too late for me to apologize. In any event, that Manichean world of oppressors and martyrs didn't exist for me anymore, if it ever had. The scenario was too monotonous. I didn't want to be part of any vicious circle anymore. I was determined to take people as they really are: human beings with their strengths and weaknesses. I couldn't put up images of political heroes on my bedroom walls, like Koffi, anymore. I no longer considered anything sacred. Idolatry was often a reaction of the desperate. I'd decided to become hopeful again, and no Africanist brotherhood on earth could work for me. That's why I knew that Mathieu, incorruptible or not, had no chance of interesting me. He hadn't told me about himself. He'd told me what he thought of himself.

Much later on, Koffi played a series of slow songs. I looked for a partner in the darkness. It wasn't easy to find one because most of the women were already on the dance floor, and the rest were in good company. Marvin Gaye was singing "Let's Get It On" in his inimitable voice. His sound was purifying the air. Couples were clutching each other ardently and, in some cases, excessively. Joseph was leaning on a woman who was heavily made up and covered in cheap jewelry. He was clinging to her like a shipwrecked man to a life preserver in the open sea. Bob was dancing alone in a corner, an imaginary guitar in his hand. Koffi had left the booth and was whispering God knows what in the ear of the owner's daughter. Her mother was shooting dirty looks at them.

It was around seven in the morning when the club closed. The house emptied slowly, the guests trickling out. Somalians, Haitians, and Jamaicans emerged nonchalantly into the pale light. There was no colour in the sky. We were walking one behind the other as if we wanted to be in one last dance train. But our silence was too heavy. It betrayed our lack of enthusiasm. It wasn't a silence of guilt; it was one of regret about leaving that underground place, that opaque world veiled in smoke, yet protective like the one before birth. The depths of the earth were also the womb of the damned. We left that telluric space reluctantly for the harsher, crueller outside world. Passersby on their way to work looked at us as if we were ghosts surprised by the light of day. We'd left somewhere as stifling as hell, but as exhilarating as a secret escape. I thought that life in Toronto should be as euphoric, but here celebration was confined to a suburban basement.

Some time later, I realized that Joseph had slipped out on us. He'd made off to his last dance partner's place. The aroma of coffee wafting out of the shops was beginning to make my mouth water.

The Prophet and the Traitor

When I woke up, squares of sunlight were scattered around my room. The Bob Marley poster, normally up on the ceiling, was now down in front of me. As the image came into focus, I recognized Bob. His head was bent over mine.

"Wake up, African!"

He handed me the telephone receiver.

"Ray? Are you still in bed? You lazybones!"

It was Maria. I gave her a reply that didn't make much sense.

"Listen, I have a favour to ask you. Can you write a love letter for me?"

I was sure I'd misunderstood.

"Raymond?"

"Yes? Did you say a love letter?"

"Yes, a love letter. That's not something I'd ask your friends. But I can ask you because I know you have some experience. I'll explain when I get there. I'll see you later."

She hung up before I could tell her I wasn't interested. Why did she want a love letter? Was it for her? I wasn't sure I understood. No, I thought, I won't write a love letter for her.

In the kitchen, Bob was making himself a sandwich. He must not have been up much before me. I could tell by the look of concentration on his face that my presence was bothering him. Even though he'd seemed more relaxed the night before, he didn't like me. He went to sit in the living room after casting a scornful glance at me. I decided to try to lighten the mood.

"Has anyone ever told you that you look like Bob Marley?"

"Yeah, I've been told that," he said curtly.

"When I woke up . . ."

"Cut the crap. You know I can't stand you," he said, eating his sandwich.

"Why? What did I do to you?"

"Personally? Nothing. But I don't trust Africans. They're the ones who sold us."

There was no sign of irritation in Bob's voice.

"What about Eddy? Don't you like him?"

"Eddy's a good guy," said Bob, smiling. "He's not an African anymore, he's a brother."

"I don't get it. What's the difference between an African and a brother?"

"Of course, you don't get it," he replied with a shrug. "You're too busy chasing after white women like Maria. The difference is that an African is willing to sell his mother to a white man. A brother couldn't do that."

Bob put on his tam and, without another word, closed the door as he left. His animosity was starting to worry me. His allusion to Maria was only an excuse. His resentment was rooted more in the past. He was so unshakable in his beliefs that confronting him wouldn't get me anywhere. I had to wait for Eddy. He'd managed to overcome Bob's prejudices and could no doubt prevent the situation from getting out of hand.

The Love Letter

Maria came to see me in the afternoon. I recognized her perfume before she entered the bedroom. She had a childlike smile on her lips. The love letter wasn't for her.

"It's for Ann Philips. She and David Lee send each other love letters in all different languages."

"Why?"

"To overcome barriers!"

"I don't really know what you mean."

Maria put her hands on her hips and heaved a sigh of irritation.

"Ann and David can't express their feelings for each other openly. Her father hates the Chinese. He thinks they're taking over Vancouver. So they want to get beyond prejudices by writing letters in different languages."

"Okay. So, it's a symbolic thing."

Ann had sent her first letter in Italian. For her, it was the sexiest language on earth. Then she asked Maria to write David a love letter in Portuguese, which Maria was happy to do. David sent Ann a letter in Cantonese, then another in Greek. Of course, they had to have the letters translated to understand them. Apparently, this was the most intense and delicious time in the whole affair. Now Ann wanted a letter in French.

"Why me? Why not Joseph, for example?"

"Well, you both speak French, but you're a sensitive guy," said Maria, pretending to look at the posters of black leaders in the room. "Besides," she added, "it pays well and I know you're broke. So, I thought of you."

"I don't know what to say. I've never written a love letter to a man."

"Well, here's your chance! Anyway, love's love."

"That's easy to say. He'll know that the letter's not from Ann. She doesn't speak French."

"Don't be ridiculous! If you think they're the ones who wrote the letters in Portuguese and Greek, you're mistaken."

"Do rich people ever like to complicate things!"

"Tsk! If rich people learned other languages, you wouldn't have any work in this country," she replied, smiling at me with a reproving look. "I'll be back in two hours."

She laid a lot of money on the table and headed for the door.

"Not so fast!" I said.

She stopped abruptly and turned her head.

"Have you ever fallen in love? I mean very deeply . . ."

She opened her mouth to speak, but I didn't give her time.

"Have you ever fallen madly in love with someone?"

She smiled, looking coy. She must have thought I was asking her a trick question, trying to learn secrets she hadn't yet revealed.

"Do you really think I can tell you everything? I'm not that naive."

"When you feel like a volcano," I added, ignoring what she'd just said.

Maria's expression changed. Her eyes took on a dark, stormy hue.

"When you love someone, you're convinced that you can change the world together, solve the planet's problems, redraw the borders of countries and oceans so that everybody's happy."

She lowered her eyelids. I could sense that she was recalling a love affair. I could see on her face the unforgettable thrill of a first kiss. I could discern on her lips the caress that left a mark on her soul.

"Maria?"

She looked at me again, her eyes filled with tears. Without a word, she left, banging the door.

Bijou, My Love

I decided to write to Bijou, but I didn't have her address. She hadn't wanted to give it to me, claiming that she'd soon be leaving the country. I wanted to write to her anyway. I thought about her too much not to tell her so. Since I didn't know how to reach her, I decided to write to the person I carried within me, the one who kept coming to me in my dreams and speaking to me in hushed tones. I didn't need an address. I'd write a letter that she'd never read, one that would express in black and white the love I had for her. I realized now that I had loved her, yet I hadn't told her. What's worse, I'd never admitted it to myself, even though every time I thought about her, I felt sad and melancholic. I had all the signs of a broken heart. This letter would help reveal to me my love gone amiss, gone unspoken. From this short note celebrating my love, I expected great enlightenment.

Dear Bijou,

I cannot endure your searing absence. The immense sorrow I feel at not being close to you burns in great darkness. The memory of your fruity lips and salty loins comes back to me in my sleep. At night, you are a strong wine and I am drunk with you. And you? Are you sad being so far away from me? Do you think about me? Do you still want me?

I often have the same dream. My temples are on fire. You emerge from the water, your hands set with crystalline pearls. You lay your palms on my face and put out the flames.

You are the only crack in my sanity that I never want to fill.

In rereading my letter, I saw that I didn't need to adapt it for Ann and David. Maria was right. One letter expressing specific love could apply to other love relationships. There were no boundaries in this area.

I set down my pen and walked over to the window. I could barely hear the hum of the traffic below. The day was captivating, the light striking. I glimpsed something extraordinary behind the sun, a supernatural radiance. For a few moments, I peered at the luminous sheet of ethereal fleece. In it, I saw flourishes in the form of angels, trumpets, and winged horses. It was true, I thought, that I had loved Bijou. I felt joyful that I'd been able to tell her so. I'd confessed everything to the one who resided in my heart.

Maria returned in the afternoon. She was in a great rush. She took the letter and made for the door, saying, "I don't have time to talk. I have to go and pick up my mother at choir practice and I'm late. She's going to kill me."

When she left me, I'd already lost the feeling of completeness the letter had given me. I'd long come back down from the elation I'd experienced. To make up for the loneliness, I promised myself that I'd go downtown the next day. To escape my bedroom, I sought the vitality of the heart of the city. I wanted to be swallowed up by Toronto, to lose myself in her streets so that I'd never return to these four walls again. I nurtured a secret hope of becoming a new person, with no past, no pain and, especially, no regrets. I would've liked the transformation to be fast and drastic. I wasn't keen on belonging to a generation of ill-adapted immigrants. Everything had to start with me—me forgetting, me beginning anew. I had to learn how to come into the world again, in the middle of North America.

That night, I felt like talking to someone about Bijou. I wanted an attentive ear, but I didn't have a confidant at the apartment. Bob was too vindictive, I didn't trust Joseph, and Koffi was never there. Besides, I didn't know how to talk about heartbreak to such dogmatic minds.

Just then, Joseph rushed into the room to get something that belonged to him. His tall, slender silhouette groped about in the darkness. I watched him in silence, wondering if he confided in Bob or

Koffi. I doubted it. I didn't find him sincere enough. He'd told me such unlikely stories. First, he was supposedly the son of a sugarcane cutter. Then there was that political family saga that had compelled him to come to Canada. Yet, he appeared totally to be from a middle-class family. His good education betrayed him. It all greatly intrigued me.

To console myself for not having anyone to talk to, I thought about a friend I'd known for a long time, in whom I used to confide everything. His name was Michel Agbessi, and he was a cultured man.

Michel Agbessi, the Artist

Michel Agbessi had a chubby face, a plump physique, and a cigarette between his lips at all times. His addiction to tobacco had caused him serious health problems. He'd even had to leave his job in the public service. Every day at noon, he would set his one-hundred-kilo body down on a moped and go for a drink at a seedy bar called Champs-Elysées. Beer flowed like water when he was there, so much so that his belly seemed to grow by the week. Michel Agbessi was kind and appreciated the good things in life. His only enemy was the African poet, Léopold Senghor, whose writing he disliked.

Agbessi was above all very endearing. When I decided to drop out of school and get by on odd jobs, he said, "You're doing the right thing, Raymond. Odd jobs won't ruin you. Look at what's become of me after twenty years of loyal service. Obedience is a cancer. Your education's elsewhere." Then he invited me to his favourite bar.

A tireless talker, Agbessi could discuss novels and paintings all night without showing any signs of fatigue. I liked that type of evening because I discovered far-off exotic landscapes thanks to his talent of distilling his knowledge. In his small apartment in the poor neighbourhood of Akpakpa, he would take on the entire world, commenting on masterpieces as if they'd been created just for him. Painting was his favourite topic. He'd always dreamt of owning an art gallery somewhere in Paris or Milan.

When he was young, he'd received a scholarship to study agronomy in Moscow. He never went there, though, explaining his decision by saying, "What did you want me to do up there? Paint kolkhozes?"

I remember a picture, *The Raft of the Medusa* by the Romantic painter Théodore Géricault, that was prominently displayed in his living room. For me, that work among his enigmatic African masks and wooden statuettes represented a window onto the West, hope for reconciling different arts with the universal.

"Look at this scene," he said, in a theatrical manner. "The frigate Medusa went down off the coast of Africa in 1816. The captain escaped, abandoning his passengers. Look at these souls in distress on this makeshift raft. Ah, Géricault is fascinating!" he declared, his eyes beaming with delight. "This work is of epic greatness!"

Not seeing me as carried away as he was, he continued emphatically, "You see these men? Blacks and whites, slaves and masters, trying to survive on a raft . . . In the end, Raymond, it all comes down to that! The only truth is that of the imagination."

Agbessi had a memory like an elephant. He'd often recite a passage from Tennessee Williams that he'd learned by heart: "Among the things love includes, unlimited as life and perhaps as death, there is demolition of self and possibly also of the object of love!"

At night, he'd start up his old crank and horn gramophone and listen to Billie Holiday. "With 'Lady Day,'" he liked to say, "things are as clear as the light of day." When he imitated her singing "Me, Myself and I" in the subdued light of his living room, his size wasn't even noticeable. He'd dance with ease, an invisible person in his arms, his pudgy hands nimbly stroking imaginary hair. Eccentric and capricious, Agbessi had an innate sense of the theatrical. He must've listened to that song so many times that he could've sung it in his sleep. "Me, myself and I have just one point of view / We are convinced there's no one else like you."

In order to support himself, Agbessi had found a juicy connection at the national lottery. Through his contacts, in exchange for a cut, he would ensure that his most generous clients hit the jackpot. It was dangerous, but so lucrative. In any event, he said that he didn't have long to live, so he had to make the most of it. Agbessi wasn't wrong on that score. His deep, phlegmy cough grew worse and he died of lung cancer, a cigarette butt still in the corner of his mouth.

For Agbessi, universal art was his earthly sustenance, his fruits of the earth. I sometimes imagine him fixing his gaze on Toronto. I can picture him taking in the wonders of the city, casting an eye on them—the eye of a passionate man for whom nothing was out of bounds. Not even men, especially not men.

News from Eddy

Koffi came home very late. He had to go out again to work as a DJ at the same club as the previous night. Before he left, he told me that Eddy had just called. Eddy knew that I was there, but he hadn't wanted Koffi to wake me up.

"I wasn't asleep," I said.

"It doesn't matter. He'll be here in a few days. Do you want to come tonight," he asked, standing in the half-open door.

"No, some other time. I'd like to sleep tonight."

I didn't manage to fall asleep, though. I was thinking about how Eddy and I had met, under strange circumstances, at a time that now belonged to the past. It was during the socialist period in Benin when a military regime, proclaiming itself revolutionary, ruled the country. A curfew was enforced at nightfall, and submachine gun fire could often be heard around the presidential palace, which had been turned into a bunker. The political tension in Cotonou was unbearable. Every public speech had to end with the slogan, "Ready for the revolution, the struggle continues!"

Despite the powerful rhetoric, there were no jobs. So how were folks to earn a living? Young people like me had to survive one way or another. All the Soviet embassy offered us were Russian courses and propagandist documentaries. Eddy and I didn't meet at the Soviet embassy, but he later admitted that he'd taken a few Russian language courses there for opportunistic reasons. Our paths crossed one night in May in Cotonou during the rainy season. Blinding flashes of lightning were tearing through the sky and gusting torrential rain was sweeping over the entire city. Despite that, it was very hot. I was waiting in line at the port for my chance to convince a docker to sell me some merchandise at half price. There were a lot of us there, soaked to the skin, waiting our turn.

Eddy was standing right in front of me. The way he seemed to be on the lookout caught my attention. He didn't trust the port wardens, who were willing to turn a blind eye to our dealings. Each person had five minutes to convince a docker to slip him some goods from Hong Kong or Taiwan. You had to promise them a generous cut, and they had to bribe the port wardens. That night, silvery branches of lightning lashed the sky and premonitory cracking rumbled across the heavens. The wardens had decided to arrest some of us to satisfy the port boss, who was complaining about the frequent theft of products from his containers. Fortunately, despite the thunderclaps and pounding of the rain on the tin roofs, Eddy heard the watchmen's hurried footsteps coming toward us. He shouted, "Run! They're coming!" to everyone waiting.

Everyone scattered. Eddy disappeared behind a row of crates, and I lost sight of him. People were running in all directions to avoid the watchmen. When I saw beams of lights searching dark corners, I thought my final hour had come. From my unlit hiding place, I could hear the manhunt out on the quay. Panic-stricken, I left my spot and started running again, this time in the horrifying maze of a warehouse with no way out. I was convinced that my life would end somewhere in that dreary depot, that my footsteps were leading me directly to the place where I'd end my days. I knew that they'd start by beating me, because that's what they did to those they caught out on the quay. I could hear the batons thumping my companions in misfortune. Their grim echoes confirmed that I wouldn't survive such a beating. Screams, resounding in my head, were rising above the storm that was battering the city. Flashlights were coming dangerously close to me as I zigzagged nonstop through that enclosed Dantean space. I was sweating, panting and trapped like a rat when a hand come out of nowhere, a hand that I took for that of God. It motioned me over. Without thinking, I ran toward that unexpected hand, which turned out to be salvatory. Eddy invited me into his container, closed the large metal door, and pressed his palm over my mouth to muffle my loud breathing.

We stayed hidden half the night in the spot that Eddy had orga-
nized. Later on, no matter how much I thanked him, he told me it was
the least he could've done.

"I would've helped the others if I could've," he said.

Eddy's real name was Melchior Kpatindé. He wanted to be an actor
so badly that people ended up calling him Eddy, after Eddy Murphy.
Like me, he earned a living by doing odd jobs. He specialized in sell-
ing arts and crafts in Haie Vive, the white neighbourhood in Cotonou.
Eddy had the gift of the gab and managed to convince a good many
people to buy one of his works.

"This sculpture," he told a customer one day, "represents the
emblem of King Ghezo, who ruled from 1818 to 1858. He was one of
the most respected kings in the Kingdom of Dahomey. He was even
respected by his enemies."

Eddy knew how to impress people. In other words, he was affable,
especially when it was in his best interest.

On days when we had nothing to sell, we cleaned the windshields
of the diplomats' cars parked downtown. The tips from some of the
ambassadors helped us through lean times.

Then one day, Eddy, who had been a friend in need, left for Canada.
He had been working as a masseur for the national boxing team for a
few weeks. When the boxers left for their training, he accompanied
them and never returned to Cotonou.

The Queen of the Streets?

The next day, as planned, I headed downtown. The weather was sunny, and even the passengers on the buses looked more cheerful than on the previous few days. After consulting the map of Toronto, I decided to go down to Queen Street because of the name. A queen street, I thought, might be one that rules over the others. When I left the subway station, I saw that Queen Street, much to my chagrin, was not a luxurious place. There were very few majestic buildings. However, the people I came across seemed to be full of energy. The cyclists reigned supreme on this narrow street set with rails. They rode at top speed, hair blowing in the wind, weaving through traffic like elusive dragonflies. The traffic was stressful and, as I walked west, I realized that I was moving faster than the packed streetcars. After watching the cyclists, I turned my attention to some arguing cab drivers. They were shouting at the top of their lungs, bawling each other out, hurling invective in every conceivable language. Further on, a man, sitting in the shadow of two buildings, was holding out his empty hand to passersby. He looked up at me with his faded blue eyes. He smelled of urine. "I haven't eaten for two days," he said, his week-old stubble unable to hide the pitiful state of his teeth. It was a sorrowful sight. I quickly rummaged through my pockets and gave him a few coins.

I didn't know that three other panhandlers were waiting up the street. The first one thanked me in a cracked voice. I gave him an ambiguous smile, that of someone feeling uncomfortable. The man seemed keen on returning the smile. I couldn't help but glance at his teeth. He didn't have many left. His mouth was a hole into which I couldn't let myself fall. The pedestrians around us seemed not to see us. I was standing beside a ghost. Passersby had sealed their hearts the way you plug your nose. I slowly realized that, one day, I could be like these people who passed by without noticing anything. Toronto was like that, too. It was a place where you could live among ghosts who ask for bread, and you ignore them.

Still further along, I saw bikers parked in front of a café. Their spotless machines glistened from handlebars to hubcaps. They, on the other hand, were dishevelled and unshaven. They wore tattoos on their exposed arms and chests. Their black bomber jackets reminded me of the cover of *Rolling Stone* magazine, which I'd often read in Cotonou.

As I continued exploring Queen Street, I noticed a large number of very different-looking people. There were punks with blue hair, and artists dressed in black and pale as death. I saw lots of shaved heads, pierced noses, perforated tongues, and boots laced up to mid-thigh. Even the shop signs reflected feats of imagination. Many were made of ill-sorted materials, such as barbed wire, rusty record players, and Christmas lights.

Queen Street liked to cultivate difference. Its store windows flaunted their cheap treasures with the irreverence of a queen without a crown. The street intended to be free-spirited in its display of clothing lines, retro furniture, and art galleries full of empty frames. The place was charged with emotion like the souls who regularly went there. Edgy souls. To be handled with caution.

Fascinated by the street, I lost track of time. I wanted to get back to the apartment well before dark. So, I left behind all these hungry, grotesque and flamboyant characters who were, in their own way, jewels in the rough.

Hello Loneliness

When I reached our building, twilight was already spreading across the sky. Everything was starting to morph into moving shadows. Up at the apartment, the television was on as usual, but the sound had been muted. Bob was playing his guitar in the unlit living room. He heard me come in, but continued fingering. The notes coming from his instrument reminded me of something, but I didn't know what. Joseph was preparing food in the dark. I asked him if he could see without the light on.

"Keep your voice down," he whispered. "Bob's rehearsing for an audition tomorrow."

I kept quiet and, as dusk deepened, I merely watched Joseph heat up food in the saucepans. In the bedroom, Koffi was recuperating from the night before. His feet were fanned out and sticking out the bottom of the blanket in which he was wrapped. When I walked in, he stirred and then lay still as before. I stretched out on the bed he had lent me, the bed that was his. I waited with open eyes for night to fall completely, to cover me like a sheet shrouding a lifeless body. This apartment was depressing me more and more. Without the liveliness of Toronto, the warmth of her concrete and all of her colourful characters, I felt the pain of having left Bijou. I knew I couldn't have stayed with her because she was so determined to marry a white man. I still regretted leaving. Lying there in the dark, I could feel her warm body right next to mine. She was taking me back to a country I'd decided to leave forever. How do you change your life, I wondered. How do you escape the past so that it no longer torments you? So that it's a balm that soothes your heart? Many people from my past were in that lightless room. They were almost palpable in the denseness of the night, there in the antechamber of America. Their presence made me nostalgic for a time when I was not happy, for a time when I did not have to be reborn.

A Merciless Dinner

The atmosphere at supper was jovial. Each of us had told a joke, and now it was Bob's turn to tell one.

"There's a black cop whose boss asks him why he decided to go into law enforcement. 'Well,' says the cop, 'I figured if I didn't want to get shot at accidentally by the police, I'd better be wearing the uniform!'"

The laughter was half-hearted. Joseph still insisted that it was a good one.

The international news came on the television. A deadly explosion had occurred in Israel. After the report, which everyone listened to attentively, the discussion turned to politics. Bob gave his opinion.

"Black people around the world should support the struggle of the Palestinians. They're an oppressed people like us. What do you think, Joe?"

"I think you're right. We should send blacks to help the Palestinians. We'll show them how we freed ourselves with our bare hands in Haiti in 1804!"

"You know," added Koffi, looking at me, "the greatest black leaders were Muslims. Malcolm X, El Hadj Omar Tall, Samori Ture . . . The Quran was written to defeat the oppressor."

"Oh, forget it," exclaimed Bob, shooting a reproachful look at me. "He's a Babylon . . . He's a white man with black skin."

My heart skipped a beat.

"Go ahead and fight for the Palestinians since you're so brave," I said. "I'm staying here. You can say what you like about the Haitian Revolution, Joseph. You weren't there. I knew a dictatorship that was called a 'revolution.' Believe me, that word should be used with a lot less pride and trust."

"Oh," retorted Bob, "we have a democrat among us."

"All I'm saying, Bob, is that with or without a revolution, I always went hungry in Cotonou. I don't have faith in the great political theorists anymore. And I'm fed up with all the politicians!"

A long silence followed. It seemed to me that the good Michel Agbessi was having a laugh somewhere in a corner of the living room. I made an effort to leave the table with my head held high.

"In any case," said Joseph, "you should know that we're still the best friends you've got in Toronto."

"Good thing you're here to remind me, because otherwise I wouldn't have known."

I went straight to my room and buried myself completely beneath the blankets, my heart hammering. I was very hot, but I didn't want to pull my head out from under the covers. I stayed there, expecting my heart to explode, my chest hurting more and more. I knew that it wasn't only because I couldn't breathe. There was also the unbearable pain of feeling like I was from another planet with people who were apparently my kind. When I was almost out of air, I heard a reedy voice singing Billie Holiday's "Long Gone Blues." "Talk to me, baby / Tell me what's the matter now / Tell me, baby, what's the matter now?" It was Michel Agbessi doing one of his famous imitations. His voice was drowning out the murmur coming from the living room. I poked my head out so I could hear his singing better, but it stopped. A cool breeze blew over my salty face. It was the salt of the sea, the salt of Bijou. Thanks to them, I had escaped the suicidal despair of being alone in the world.

Brother Koffi to the Rescue

Koffi came into the bedroom later on. He opened up his mattress as usual and lay down.

"Ray?"

"Mmm . . ."

"Are you asleep?"

"No."

"Sorry about tonight. Bob and Joseph are too. We didn't mean to . . ."

"It's okay."

"You know, I've heard you talk in your sleep."

"What've I said?"

"Nothing much. Just the names of people I don't know."

He changed his position on the mattress.

"I know you never listen to me when I talk to you at night," he said. "It doesn't matter, though. The truth is, I'm not talking to you, I'm talking to myself. When I turn off the light, I can tell myself the history of my people. I can reinvent as much as I like because there's no one left now. Where have all the heroes gone? Their education's finally conquered our minds, Brother. Three hundred years in North America. They've replaced the whip with brainwashing. It's clean and quiet."

"Why does Bob resent me?"

"Oh, Bob doesn't really resent you. He lost a friend recently. Trouble with the cops. He's hurting. You have to understand that. He's not the same, Brother. When you live here, you're not the same. You'll change, too."

"That's up to me."

"Maybe, Ray. Maybe."

Koffi still played his music. That night, it was Jimmy Cliff, singing "Many Rivers to Cross."

Bob's Grief

When I woke up, I noticed that Koffi's bed was empty. He must have been gone for quite some time. I got up and stretched, feeling that I wasn't alone in the room. Bob was looking out the window, motionless, a can of beer in his hand.

"Have you been here for long?"

"No," he said, still looking outside. "I like to look at the buildings from this window. I love the way they tower over those tiny passersby down there. Those people are so small."

Bob raised his hand to lift a ringlet from his face. His voice, usually melodious, was gravelly, his tone almost cold.

"Sometimes I stay at this window for hours to see if the buildings will move . . . That's stupid, eh?"

He made as if to face me, but changed his mind.

"I really wish I could bring these goddamn concrete giants to life. Like those people who bend spoons with nothing but their minds."

"Why?"

"Because might is right. Because if these buildings were alive, they could get revenge for my friend's death . . . my brother's death."

He took a gulp of beer in silence and turned toward me. His eyes were red, his face furrowed with wrinkles I'd never seen. There was something distinctive about his suffering. He couldn't have been comforted with words: his grief was stronger than any expression of solace. His pain was deep, his wound aching slowly and endlessly.

Bob sat down beside me. His voice barely audible, he told me about his friend Harvey. He had played with him at bars in the city. They were starting to make a name for themselves. In the early hours one morning, when Harvey was going home after performing at a bar, the police signalled him to pull over. They saw him get out of his car with a case in his hand. It was his trumpet case. They ordered him to put his hands up, which he did. As the police were approaching him, he started to shake all over. One of the officers, who had a gun in his hand, pulled the trigger. Harvey had been having an epileptic fit.

Bob closed his eyes and tears ran down his cheeks. He cursed the entire world, clenching his fists in anger, grimacing with rage. He stood up abruptly and turned to the window.

"That filthy cop got nothing but a reprimand! One line of criticism in his file. That's all!"

He rested his forehead against the cold bedroom wall.

"That son of a bitch gets up every morning, kisses his wife and kids, and goes on with his police routine as if nothing ever happened. Harvey's dead. And every morning I wonder why his killer's alive."

He turned toward me. I glimpsed his creased forehead, partly hidden by his messy locks.

"Apparently, it was a mistake. He fit the description of a suspect . . . Yeah, sure! All blacks look alike."

Now I understood why he was always looking for confrontation. He'd lost his friend. And me, wanting to discover my country of refuge . . . I was a traitor. For Bob, I had no right to open my arms to this city. After all, it was in Toronto that Harvey was murdered. The place reeked of inequality and injustice.

I clasped Bob to my chest, wanting to ease his pain, trying in my own way to remove the cancer that was eating away at his soul. The flashes of fury in his eyes were hotter than any human warmth. I hadn't known Harvey, but I knew all about the rage of the oppressed. I knew the feeling of powerlessness in the face of a cold, scornful oppressor. All I had to do was draw on my experience as an African who'd known nothing but a dictatorship, to recall the smell of gunpowder and blood.

Bob sat down on the bed again. He wiped his tears with the back of his hand.

"You know, I don't really have anything against you."

His head was bent.

"I didn't want any new friends. When you came here, I felt as if someone would try to replace Harvey. I couldn't accept that. You landed here with a smile on your face . . . like a tourist in the middle of a war. It was too much for me."

"I understand."

He stood up without looking at me. Before he left, he said, "Don't tell the others that I cried."

Downtown With Maria

M aria came by to visit me the next day. She had good news for me.

"Ann had your letter translated. She told me that David's going to love it. So, you do know how to write to men!" she said, winking at me.

"Are you sure that's a compliment?"

"Since when don't you trust me?"

"Okay, never mind."

"Hmm, you're not in a very good mood this morning. We'll fix that," she announced, kissing me on the cheek. "You could use a good haircut. Come with me. I know a place that'll give you one."

"What'll we do afterwards?" I asked playfully.

"I don't know. I'm free all day."

When it came to leaving the apartment, I was ready to follow the devil.

Downstairs, children were playing ball. It was a beautiful, cool day. Maria didn't have her red Corvette: she was driving a royal blue Miata. It was a two-door with rounded, almost sensual curves.

"I sent my car in to the garage to have it serviced. I'm renting this one and I'm starting to like it. I might even buy one."

There was almost no one out on the balconies to admire us. Maria could see the disappointment on my face.

"Wait a second, we'll get them out."

She lowered our windows and raised the volume of the radio. The music that was playing nearly burst my eardrums. Half the balconies filled at once.

"You see that! All you have to do is wake them up!"

Our car disappeared amid whistling from the onlookers.

The hairdresser that Maria had in mind was located in the south end of the city. To get there, we drove along suburban streets that all looked alike. The roughcast on high-rises was peeling and spotted with pigeon droppings. The birds had congregated on a number of balconies and seemed to have made their nests there. At the foot of buildings and factories, I could see fluorescent graffiti between fresh layers of dried cement: "I love John," "Metallica," "Prince and The Boyz." The colours were still vivid. The letters embodied something brutal and icy: a silent rebellion.

We came across enormous bins full of garbage on street corners. When our car got too close to one of them, hungry gulls let out sinister cries. Maria, who was speeding along as usual, turned down the music so we could hear each other. Our route was interspersed with huge, flat shopping malls, their advertising bills failing to brighten up their lots. There were more empty shopping carts in front of the stores than parked cars. The caddies were moving unattended between the vehicles, as if pushed by an invisible force.

As we started getting closer to downtown, the streets became narrower and the pedestrians more numerous. The traffic returned to the gripping pace of the metropolis. Maria slowed down and asked,

"What kind of a haircut do you want to get?"

"I have no idea. No, actually, I do know. I want to shave it all off."

"Shave it all off? Why? Don't you like your hair?"

"No, it's not that. I just think it'd be cool, that's all."

"I don't think you have the right head for it."

"Don't you?"

"No. But you should ask the hairdresser. He'll advise you."

We finally came to a stop.

"Well, here we are. I'm not going in. Too many men . . . I'm allergic, you know."

"Are you sure about this place?"

"Oh, there he goes doubting me again. This is where Joseph and his friends come to get their hair cut. Don't shave your head, okay?"

"Okay. I'll do something else."

As she was pulling away, she shouted that she'd be back before long.

Community Meeting Place

I walked into the hairdresser without knowing what awaited me: a room packed with people who were talking and calling out to each other constantly. Almost everyone turned toward me—the newcomer—and inspected me from head to toe. Then the murmur of voices resumed with renewed vigour, the busy hairdressers returning to their work. All of us at the salon were black; the only woman was the cashier, who was pretending to read a book amid the racket. The space was about fifteen metres long. The clients settled in styling chairs were facing horizonal mirrors, where their images repeated endlessly as in an Andy Warhol painting. Other clients, sitting behind white-smocked hairdressers, were flipping through magazines while waiting their turns. I went and sat down despite the sidelong glances. When I lifted my head, I saw Koffi's leaders displayed on the walls: Marcus Garvey in full regalia, then Malcolm X and Martin Luther King shaking hands. They were surrounded by African flags. This place wasn't just a hairdresser. I'd stumbled into one of the nerve centres of black consciousness in Toronto. A sign appearing above the mirrors read, "Clients and staff are asked not to use indecent or coarse language."

I was no longer too sure what I'd walked into. The hubbub was gradually making me feel dizzy. Electric clippers were droning in and out incessantly in a sort of infernal fanfare. I started to look at the floor to stop my head from spinning, but it appeared unstable. It was steadily inundated with black hair raining down. Archipelagos of black foam stood out here and there against the white surface.

"Hey, Peter! Got anything to snack on?" called a voice from the back.

A man pointed to where the food was located. The strong smell of hair lotion emanated from the sinks, whose open mouths were waiting for heads of hair to straighten. A television perched on the wall at the rear was transmitting images of a cricket game, but no one seemed to be paying attention. Even the radio, playing deafening music, couldn't drown out the chatter. What were all these people managing to say to each other in such a clamour? Meanwhile, wave after wave of black foam continued to cover the floor. It all made me feel increasingly queasy. Finally, a hairdresser called me over in an authoritative tone.

"What kind of cut do you want?" he asked tersely.

"Any kind," I replied just as tersely.

He looked at me, amazed.

"Something quick and simple."

He put a smock on me that was not as white as his own and picked up his conversation with the neighbouring hairdresser where he'd left off. He didn't speak to me again.

I felt more and more nauseous. The smell of food and straightening creams was making me sick. The hairdresser cut my hair very short and by the time he'd finished, I was quite pale. He sent me to the cash without another word. I paid and left in a hurry.

Outside, I sat down on the sidewalk for a few moments, to give myself time to recover.

"What's wrong?" asked Maria, who had come to pick me up.

"Don't know . . . Don't feel well."

She helped me into the car.

"You can't go home like this. I'm taking you to see a doctor!"

"No, no. I'll be all right. Just need to rest a little. That's all."

"If you'd at least tell me what's wrong . . . maybe I could help!" she said, irritated.

"I don't know. Just feel dizzy, I guess."

"Well, what happened?"

Maria saw my dazed expression and understood that I wouldn't talk about it. Only she wanted to know more.

"Listen, you've just ruined my day. So, either you tell me what made you dizzy or we go to see the doctor."

"Okay. No point in getting worked up. The hair salon . . . it was the hair salon."

"But ... what's wrong with the hair salon? The place is fine! Besides..."

"Besides what?" My eyes challenged her to follow through with her thought.

"I thought you'd feel like you were with family... you know, comfortable."

She turned off her car engine and took off her sunglasses.

"Did the hair salon make you feel this way, Ray?"

"It's not a hair salon, Maria. It's a community centre."

"And so, you're allergic to community centres?"

"No. But I don't think the smell of rice is right in a place like that!"

"You mean they eat there?" she exclaimed, staring at me wide-eyed.

"Yes. I don't know about you, but rice with shaving cream doesn't sit well with me."

Maria gaped at me for a second or two. I could see that she was trying to keep a straight face, but she didn't manage to. She exploded with laughter and howled on and on. Pedestrians turned round to see who was roaring. The little Miata even shook somewhat.

When she finished, I asked her what she'd found so funny.

"You, Ray! You're not like other guys!"

"You mean other black guys?"

"Yeah. You're not like Joseph at all. I've never heard of a black who can't stand the smell of rice. You're really different. And I like that," she was quick to add.

Maria had no idea of the anger she'd just sparked in me. Her off-hand remark was unbearably revealing. It incensed me to hear her talk about me as rare. She was unaware of all the other people who must have found the salon as stifling as me but said nothing for fear of offending someone. I was all the more furious because she'd complimented me on my reaction. I felt that her comments were condescending in the extreme. I pressed my lips together to avoid shouting right in her face. A fleeting glint appeared in my eyes, as bright as a blade in the sun.

"Now that you're feeling better, would you like to go for a drink?"

she asked, not suspecting my outrage.

"You know, you're not like other women either. You're really peculiar."

"What does that mean?" she cried, a foreboding look in her eyes.

"You sleep with someone before inviting him for a drink. Is that a common quirk among white women?"

Maria, who had started driving, slammed on the brakes in the middle of traffic. There was a series of screeches. We even heard one car hit another behind us. Insults exploded like firecrackers from all around. Maria spewed a litany of profanities in Portuguese until she was breathless.

"Get out of my car! Beat it! Now! Before I call the police!"

Abuse was being hurled from every vehicle driving around us.

Maria grabbed me by the collar, crumpling my shirt and choking me.

"Get out or I'll scratch your eyes out!"

I was convinced that she'd do it. I climbed out of the car without a word. I heard the tires of the Miata squeal behind me. Then all that remained was the innocuous sound of car engines on the street.

Later, as I travelled back to the apartment, I had time to think over what had happened. You had to be terrified of the rest of the world to shut yourself up for hours at a hair salon, turned into a makeshift restaurant and conversation room. Only people deprived of freedom stayed in such stifling places. Those blacks didn't feel free. Toronto was a prison without bars. I regretted losing my temper with Maria. She was much dearer to me than all the blacks in the city. She shared her joys and sorrows with me. She was more genuine than my roommates. No one was worth our tearing each other to pieces over. I was sure that I'd killed our friendship. I was convinced that I'd never see her again. At the end of the day, I was the one who was the most terrified in the world.

Back to Square One

I walked through the apartment door, sure that I was going to die of loneliness there. All that awaited me were political posters on the walls and a bed that didn't belong to me. I didn't have a cent left to escape the place, and I expected to stay in my room long enough to croak from nostalgia. My memories of Africa were going to be my only thoughts—thoughts that would torment me.

Joseph was in the living room, dialing a number.

"Hey, Raymond!"

He motioned me to join him. It was impossible for me to talk to him at that moment. I opened the bedroom door and turned to him in silence. We stood there staring at each other for a few seconds. Seeing my tormented expression, Joseph decided to keep quiet. The slightest comment from him and I would have told him to get lost. He must have sensed that I was about to explode.

"Leave me alone! This isn't the time!" I shouted.

I slammed the door and collapsed on the bed. Lying there, I realized that I was exhausted from all the confrontation and ploys. This week had been the most difficult of my life. I was looking for a relationship without all the distrust. Something I was sure of. A look that wouldn't leave me wondering what the person was thinking. I was anxious to see Eddy again. I needed his help, his outstretched hand. The same one that rescued me that horrific night in Cotonou. Why was he waiting to get in touch with me? Why hadn't he asked Koffi to wake me up the other night when he called? He must have known that I was dying to speak to him.

I tried to doze off, so I'd stop thinking about all these questions. I didn't manage to, though. Eddy's silence worried me. What was he living on? Had he given up his ambition of becoming an actor? I was afraid of the answer. I knew that if Eddy had abandoned his dream, it would be a great failure for him, maybe the greatest ever. I also knew that his potential success would encourage me to pursue my own dreams, however vague they might be.

I couldn't get to sleep, so I decided to sit up on the bed. As I was doing so, I heard a knock.

"Who is it?"

Joseph half-opened the door and poked his head through.

"It's Eddy. He's on the phone."

"Eddy?"

"Yes," replied Joseph, opening the door wider.

I felt awkward for being so curt with him earlier. I stood up without looking at him, still feeling very embarrassed. I brought the receiver feverishly to my ear.

"So, Raymond! How are you?"

It was his voice all right. He was calling from Montreal. I didn't know where to start.

"Eddy? You sure took your time to get in touch!"

"Oh, come on! Is that all you have to say to me after all these years?"

"No! I'm really happy to hear from you! Are you okay?"

"Yes! More than okay! I just landed a role in a movie that'll be shot in Montreal!"

"Congratulations!" I exclaimed. "I'm . . ."

I couldn't find the words to tell him over the phone how thrilled I was.

"Is that why you haven't been in touch? Because you wanted to surprise me?"

"Yes! I asked Joseph and the others not to say anything about why I'd gone to Montreal. I wanted to tell you myself in person. I thought I'd be back sooner, but I got delayed by the contracts I had to sign and all the paperwork. I'll be in Toronto tomorrow."

"You can't imagine how happy your call makes me!"

Eddy laughed on the other end.

"I haven't landed the role of a lifetime yet, so I can't afford to talk for long."

"No problem."

"I gather you've met my friends?"

"Hmm, yep . . ."

"Oh, don't worry. They won't bite. And I hope you won't either," he added in a jesting tone. "Give yourselves time to get to know each other. Damn, Raymond. It's great to hear your voice."

When I hung up, everything had changed for me. I took the long-corded phone back into the living room, and returned to the bedroom with the hope that one day I could do something with my life. I was convinced I could reinvent myself, thanks to the hope that Eddy had just given me with his good news, and especially with his enthusiastic voice and hearty laughter. I understood that even if he never made it big in such a difficult line of work, he'd overcome despair for good. He was the master of his fate, and I had to become the master of mine.

The Invitation

Joseph had left an envelope on my bed. My name was written on it. There was no stamp, and I didn't recognize the writing. I opened it, very intrigued by the whole mystery. It was an invitation from Ann Philips. She was organizing a little party in honour of her mother's departure for Vancouver. Joseph returned to the bedroom.

"So, what did he say?"

"He said that we need to take time to get to know each other."

"That's true."

Joseph came over to me and extended his hand.

"My name's Joseph Dorsinville. What's yours?"

I put my hand in his and replied, "Raymond Dossougbé."

"We haven't seen each other for ages . . . centuries, in fact," he said, smiling. Then we both burst out laughing so we wouldn't look ridiculous.

"By the way, who brought the letter here?" I asked, showing him Ann's invitation.

"Maria. She came by barely an hour ago."

I waited for him to say more, but nothing came. He was about to walk out of the bedroom when I asked, "Didn't she leave a message for me?"

"No."

Joseph departed without another word. I picked up the envelope and read the invitation again. I discovered that there was a note on the back: "You'd better accept Ann's invitation for tomorrow night if you want to see me again. If you don't . . . well, too bad for you." It was signed "Maria."

That night when Koffi and Bob came home, we all went out for a drink together. To raise a glass to Eddy's good news, to raise a glass to friendship.

The Abandoned Guitarist

The day went by slowly. I decided to read a book about the life of Marcus Garvey. It explained his great ambition: to take the black American diaspora back to the promised land, back to Africa. His call for a return to Africa failed. What's more, millions of blacks today don't know who Marcus Garvey was.

I stopped reading from time to time to listen to Bob play. He was practising in the next bedroom, fingering the strings with strength and precision. There was something tropical about the notes. No voice was accompanying him, no trumpet either. I imagined the cries of children playing in a yard. I thought of women crushing millet, their foreheads glistening in the beating sun. The rhythm of their pestles would have paired well with Bob's guitar. He was alone within four cold walls, the abandoned guitarist.

The Grey-Eyed Véronique

The afternoon finally came to an end, and I left my room with the hope of overcoming my melancholy. Someone knocked on the apartment door. It was Joseph, his arms loaded with plastic bags. Maria was with him, her arms full as well.

"You've got two men here who aren't doing a damn thing, and I'm helping you carry the bags of groceries up! Don't you think that's a bit much, Joe?"

"Relax, Sweetheart! I wanted you to come up. I want to cook for you."

"Hi, Ray. Ready for tonight?"

She gave me a peck on the cheek.

"Yeah, I'm ready. Well almost."

I hadn't changed my clothes yet.

"Make yourself comfortable," said Joseph, motioning Maria to an armchair.

The guitar could still be heard from the bedroom. Maria sat down, ran her fingers through her hair, and crossed her legs. She was wearing a multicoloured floral summer dress that hardly reached her knees. Her bare, freshly shaven calves were almost olive in colour. Her spicy perfume was mixed with her perspiration. Carrying the bags of groceries had winded her.

"A beer, please."

"Coming right up, Dear," said Joseph, who had started to cook.

Maria gave me an amused look. She pretended to be annoyed by Joseph's overly attentive attitude. Bob came out of his room.

"Oh, it's my dear Maria! How did you come today? In a Corvette or a Porsche?"

"Don't pay any attention to him," said Joseph with an uneasy smile. "He's jealous."

Joseph returned to his cooking after shooting Bob a reproachful look. Bob acted as if he hadn't noticed a thing.

"Don't worry, Bob. When you're rich and famous, we'll talk about my Corvette."

Joseph laughed too exuberantly. The conversation was making him uncomfortable.

"Well, you got me there, Maria. I give up," conceded Bob, throwing up his hands.

"Not so fast, Brother! I was starting to like you," she said, giving him a suggestive smile.

"Sorry, I'm out of fuel."

"Oh, that's too bad. I was counting on you to fill my tank."

This time, Bob laughed. Maria took a sip of beer, her eyes leaving Bob and settling on me.

"And you? Don't you have anything to criticize me for?"

"Yes, your dress. It's not short enough."

Joseph laughed nervously as he continued cooking. There was a knock on the door. Maria got to her feet before all of us.

"I'll get it! I'll play hostess while a man is doing the cooking."

When she opened the door, her playful, provocative attitude gave way to surprise, then arrogance.

"Suis-je bien chez Joseph Dorsinville?" asked a woman with a Caribbean accent, but Parisian intonation.

"Zorry, I don't speak Frrrench . . ." said Maria. "Jo-Zeph?"

The visitor signalled Joseph to the door with a curt gesture. He rushed over to her, looking panic-stricken. His eyes had widened as if to get a better view. Maria walked slowly back to her chair, scraping the floor with her high heels.

"Who's that bitch?" she asked me between clenched teeth.

"Véronique?" exclaimed Joseph, almost gasping in amazement.

"Holy!" blurted Bob, revitalized. The evening promised to be interesting.

"Come in! I didn't know when you were coming to Toronto. What a nice surprise!"

Véronique was about thirty. She was wearing thick lipstick, had a firm chest and an hour-glass figure. She planted a wet kiss on Joseph's cheek.

"How are you, Darling? Oh, you've gained weight! You'll have to go on a diet. It's all the junk food they sell in this country. You'll soon be unrecognizable."

She inspected the apartment, her grey eyes peering out from her oval face.

"Ah! The student life. It's pitiful."

Joseph choked on his saliva, then cleared his throat as if he intended to speak. Véronique looked at each of us in turn. She was very beautiful. Her straightened black hair was pulled back into a tight bun. Her Creole earrings gave her an air of nobility. Her smile was friendly, but she ignored Maria.

"How are you?" she asked all of us.

Bob stood up and embraced her. She let him do so.

"Welcome, Sister. Joseph's told us a lot about you. And he wasn't lying."

She smiled and turned to me.

"Bob, you devil! You'll never change," said Joseph.

He motioned Bob to keep an eye on the pots on the stove.

"This is Raymond Dossou . . . um . . . sorry, Ray. I have trouble pronouncing African names."

"That's okay. I'm Raymond Dossougbé," I said, getting to my feet and extending my hand. She shook it with a certain politeness.

Maria was watching Véronique out of the corner of the eye. There was something luminous about the biracial woman's brown skin, a sort of lactescence.

"I'm Maria. I'm Joseph's ex and love Haitian men."

Her unexpected introduction cast quite a chill. Joseph scratched his chin. Bob broke into laughter and so did Maria. Everyone else was quick to follow suit to conceal their uneasiness. The musician, thanks to his reaction, had prevented an all-out fight.

When everyone sat down at the table, Joseph talked about Canada.

He mentioned how difficult it was to live in a cold country. Véronique, who was doing her best to avoid looking at Maria, laid her left hand with polished nails on Joseph's forearm.

"Don't worry. When you finish school, you can come back to Haiti . . . The sacrifice will have been worth it."

Joseph lowered his eyes and emptied his glass of water in one gulp. Maria finished her beer while pretending to watch a documentary on television. Bob was eating with great gusto. Nothing seemed to be bothering him.

"How long do you plan to stay?"

"Just a week. I have some commitments in New York."

Joseph squirmed in his chair and ended up speaking to Véronique in Creole. She responded with a polite smile. They both excused themselves and went into Bob's bedroom to talk. While they were gone, Maria reminded me that we had to leave soon. I was about to get changed when Véronique emerged from the bedroom. Her furrowed brow and lips twisted into a snarl did not bode well. She slammed the bedroom door, almost catching Joseph's fingers in it, bumped into me in the hallway, and marched into the living room without looking back. She snatched her leather handbag. Joseph, understanding that she intended to leave, rushed in front of her.

"Oh, come on, listen to me *doudou à moué!*"[1]

He tried to hold her back.

"*Pinga touché mouin, pinga!*"[2]

"*Doudou!*"[3]

"Whatever you do, don't call me that! All those letters where you said you were in school. You dirty liar!"

Véronique shook her head in disgust.

"That'll teach me to trust a good-for-nothing."

Maria sputtered with laughter. The biracial woman shot her a murderous look.

---

1   My darling!
2   Don't you dare touch me!
3   Darling!

"Shut up, you little slut. You've probably slept with the whole household."

Maria was on her feet so quickly that no one had time to intervene. She'd already laid her hands on Véronique.

"You know what I do to little show-offs like you?" said Maria, clutching her by the throat.

Véronique did not, however, back down. She freed herself from Maria's grip and retorted, "We know what you little white girls are like! You play the virgin then screw like rabbits, lusting after black men!"

Without a word, Maria seized Véronique by the neck again and started to tighten her grasp. Joseph, overwhelmed by the situation, begged us to do something right away. We managed to grab hold of Maria, and Joseph of Véronique. The two women were insulting each other with unparalleled vulgarity in their mother tongues. Véronique tried to claw Maria, who was showing the Haitian her behind. Joseph managed to restrain Véronique, but it cost him: she dug her nails into his arm for preventing her from harpooning Maria. He howled, which did nothing to help matters.

"That's my food you have in your stomach, you anemic little black girl! I've been feeding your man, you tart!"

"Your slop's for animals, you whore! You low-class hooker!"

To prevent one of the women from charging at the other, Joseph decided to leave the apartment with Véronique. That didn't stop Maria from continuing to insult her after she left.

Just as Joseph and Véronique were going out the door, Koffi was coming in. He was surprised to see the strange woman leaving his place.

"Did I miss something?" he asked, a smile on his lips.

No one replied.

"Maria, you look fit to be tied. What's going on?"

Bob took Koffi aside and whispered something in his ear. Koffi listened attentively, nodding.

"Come on, Raymond, we're leaving. We're going to be late for Ann's party."

I didn't have time to change into something dressier. I dashed into my room to get a clean shirt and kept the same jeans on. Maria was in no mood to wait. When I came back out into the living room, Koffi was calming her down.

"My dear, you shouldn't get all worked up about this. We blacks are polygamous by nature. It's an ancestral thing. You're like a sister, you can understand that. In my ancestors' countries, it's the wife who chooses her husband's next woman."

"But I'm not going out with Joseph anymore! We're just friends!" said Maria, exasperated.

That didn't stop Koffi, now that he'd gotten started. He stretched out his long, muscular legs to make himself comfortable.

"A woman who helps us with the groceries is a sister! Isn't that right, guys?"

"Oh, yes!" replied Bob and I at the same time.

"A sister who worries about us when we don't have food in our stomachs is a real sister. Am I wrong?"

"No, you're right."

"Am I lying?"

"No, you're telling the truth."

Our answers were almost synchronized. Bob and I were trying to follow the rhythm of Koffi's questions.

"I know sisters who wouldn't do what you do for us. Do you doubt that?"

"No."

"Am I wrong?"

"No, you're right."

Bob gave me a complicit smile. We were enjoying ourselves all the more because Maria was going along with it. I didn't know if she didn't mind our ploy or if she was secretly taking pleasure in it. In any event, it seemed to be working. She relaxed, especially when Koffi took out a joint. After a few puffs, she had cheered up completely.

"Okay, Brothers, anyone who wants to come with me is welcome!"

We followed her out the door like three thieves happy with our heist. The night owls on their balconies saw three black men get into a red Corvette driven by a woman whose laughter was too loud to be natural. We quickly disappeared into the starlit night under the beams of the white streetlights.

Ties that Bind or Betrayal?

We pulled up in front of Ann's apartment in one piece. Maria, although stoned and tipsy, had handled the car as if she were sober. The building was steeped in darkness and dotted with subdued lights on almost every floor. Across the street, Lake Ontario was more illuminated, pleasure boats covering the water's smooth, pearly surface. The air was much cooler and cleaner here than in the grey suburbs at Jane and Finch. Even at night, you could feel that nothing rotted of boredom or poverty in this place. I breathed in that pure breeze as if it were the last. Most of the building's well-to-do residents had gone to bed. Their vitality and confidence in the future permeated the night air. A few easygoing passersby, laughing, content with their day, were making their way down toward the lake.

Maria was looking irritated again.

"What's wrong now?" I asked, in a tone that barely concealed my annoyance with her mood swings.

"This is all your fault," she replied. "Why did you have to make eyes at my best friend's mother? Do you know the risk I'm taking in showing up at this bourgeois place with three . . . black men as tall as hydro poles?"

I told Bob and Koffi to wait for us there by the elevator on the ground floor. They weren't happy, but they complied. Koffi turned to me and said,

"Brother Ray, keep cool with the little white woman."

"Trust me," I replied with a friendly smile.

"I wouldn't want to see your picture in their crap newspaper tomorrow morning," he said, turning on his heel.

Maria was redoing her lipstick.

"I'd like to remind you that you're the one who introduced me to the Philipses. Why don't you tell the truth? You're jealous. You're afraid I'll steal all the attention."

"That's not why!"

She put her makeup bag away.

"The Philipses aren't used to seeing so many black men. And neither are their guests!"

"You mean that when we walk in, they're all going to put their hands up and say, 'Take everything we have, but spare our lives!'"

"Yeah, probably," she said. "Stop looking at me like I'm a member of the Ku Klux Klan. I'm not the one who invented racism. You don't know rich people. You're from Africa. The richer they are, the less . . . tolerant they are."

"Maria, this is absurd. I'm not the one who drove Bob and Koffi here in my Corvette. So I'll wait for you here and watch you tell them that they're not welcome at the Philips's."

Maria remained silent and assessed the situation.

"Why won't you admit that you wanted them to come? You're being a hypocrite!"

"You're the hypocrite!"

She eyed the pair of friends who were waiting in front of the elevator. They looked like something was eating them, especially Bob. Maria sighed and gestured that she'd given in. We rode the elevator in gloomy silence. Maria stopped once more in the hallway to fix her hair in front of a window. When Ann's apartment door opened, she'd already found her smile again—a smile full of feigned cheer. Ann kissed her on both cheeks. She was surprised to see Maria accompanied by three strapping fellows, who surrounded her like bodyguards.

"These are Raymond's friends," Maria was quick to say.

"Brothers," corrected Koffi.

Ann took him at his word.

"Come in!"

There were about ten guests in the living room. The space was large enough to accommodate them without it seeming crowded. The well-dressed couples looked at the new batch of guests as the eccentric component of the party. Whispers were uttered and throats were cleared. The elevator music hardly concealed people's surprise.

"Welcome to the Babylons!" muttered Bob. "Rich but . . . don't know how to dance. They must still be discussing investments."

The musician made his way toward a group of people who were watching him from a distance.

"Good evening. I'm Bob."

"Nice dreads!" said a blond-haired man wearing a tie.

Bob thanked him and replied, "Do you know how to make them? Here, I'll tell you."

Koffi went over to the buffet first. The table was laden with food, but no one seemed to be interested in it. He poured himself some champagne and helped himself to three caviar canapés. Then he joined some guests, who were clearly amazed by his athletic build. They took him for an American football player that one of them had seen on television. Koffi didn't waste any time in working his favourite topic into the conversation: his origins.

I ate a few salmon canapés. When I took my first sip of champagne, I felt a hand on my shoulder. It was Elizabeth Philips. She raised her glass.

"Congratulations."

Her face had been made up with finesse, so as to enhance her features.

"What for?"

My surprise amused her. My eyes ventured to the edge of her bodice. She was wearing a low-cut black silk dress, with a brooch close to her bust: a jaguar set with white crystals. Despite her hand on my shoulder, she maintained the air of a magnate's wife.

"For convincing Maria to bring your brothers!"

"Oh! You know her well, then."

"Maybe better than she thinks."

That last comment dissipated in the friendly atmosphere of the party.

"Come with me. I'll introduce you to some friends."

As I followed her, Mrs Philips told me to call her by her first name.

She introduced me to an architect and his wife. The husband was of retirement age and his wife was thirty years younger. Elizabeth told them that I was a friend of her daughter and that I was from Mozambique. She went on, without batting an eyelid, to explain that Ann had met me at a café, where I worked as a waiter. Of course, I had ambition. I wanted to be an engineer. I merely smiled, so much so that the couple must have wondered if I spoke English fluently. They didn't ask.

Koffi wanted Ann to show him her music collection.

"Not bad. But I think we'll have to do better if we want to wake up your guests."

In truth, Koffi found Ann's choice of music very boring.

"I brought a few CDs with me . . . Do you mind if I play them?"

Ann agreed without hesitation. The whole situation was so out of the ordinary for her. She noticed Koffi's strong arms when he rolled up his sleeves.

"What gym do you go to?"

Koffi smiled as he continued to pull CDs out of his leather jacket.

"Oh, it's all natural. I've never set foot in a gym. There's no secret, my dear. It's in the blood."

Ann blushed slightly then moved away.

Koffi put on some reggae music with African drums. Bob stopped in the middle of a conversation about the different properties of coconut milk.

The brunette with whom he'd been speaking accepted his invitation to dance with some trepidation. Bob danced very energetically, circling her like a lasso ready to tighten. She gave a flirty laugh. She liked the musician very much and was captivated by the tossing of his tresses. Koffi moved the furniture back to give them more room. Other guests started to dance as well, trying to follow the rhythm as best they could. Bob's partner was moving more and more lasciviously, swaying her hips.

"That's it, let yourself go!" urged Bob.

Those who remained standing or sitting were enjoying the show.

The men were watching the brunette, and the women were looking at Bob, who was as supple as a liana vine.

Elizabeth motioned me to follow her discreetly. Her evening dress had slits up the sides, and the curve of her calves made me long to caress them. I was eyeing the movement of her shapely hips when she glanced over her shoulder to ensure that I was behind her. My mouth was watering as I followed her. She went into the kitchen, which was deserted. There were dirty dishes everywhere: on the counter, on the table, in the sink. The smells in the room were making me hungry, but my appetite also had something to do with Elizabeth. She held out a pepper pâté canapé to me, which I swallowed greedily. She laughed, with her hand over her mouth, then looked at her fingers covered with pâté, and licked them slowly without a word. Her long polished nails reminded me of Veronique's. She gave me another glass of champagne, but took it back before I'd finished it.

"You have to know how to make the pleasure last," she said in a tone of mock reproach.

Then she led me into the bathroom, closed the door, and pressed her back against the tiled wall. I smelled soap, lavender and toothpaste as her hands undid my black jeans. She began caressing my sex slowly, which was not what I would've expected from a tycoon's wife. That said, I was experiencing what I'd been dreaming about since the day I met her. I could feel her warm breath on the tip of my member. I could hear her ragged breathing. Shivers ran through my body, my hunger intense. I let out a moan of pleasure.

We heard the reggae music come to an end and people clap. I was tasting my hostess when the next piece started to play: "Sexual Healing" by Marvin Gaye. The music reached us slowly as if passing down a long, deep canal, the notes penetrating our bodies like a passion elixir. We were blinded by our desire, our moist hands searching each other. I decided to undo her dress after thinking about tearing it. She was eager to help me. We sucked each other, bit each other. Elizabeth and I wanted to climb to the top of the world. Her body, much whiter than Maria's, had a delicious lightness to it, and she was easy to handle. The whimpers coming from the back of her throat were arousing me more and more. Her privates were fleecy, black and wet. I penetrated her, feeling as if I was entering a velvet jungle. Her pear-shaped breasts, somewhat slackened, began to shake with the thrusting of my pelvis to the rhythm of the music. Footfalls could be heard. Someone was nearing the door. Clinging to each other, we had difficulty coming to a stop. The handle turned, but the person couldn't enter. Elizabeth had locked the door without my noticing.

"Shit! There's someone in there."

It was Maria's voice. As soon as she left, we continued, our love-making becoming increasingly intense. Elizabeth raised her eyes to me and let her blue gaze sink into mine. Her jaw tight, she grabbed a tuft of my hair and kissed me forcefully. Her nails dug into my upper back, and I winced with pain, my pleasure growing at the same time. She closed her eyes, savouring each moment, her tense muscles softening. I felt her raining deep within, and I followed closely after her. My last thrust heralded the apocalypse of my senses, my climax releasing my being through the narrows of my body.

The silence that followed was steeped in affinity. My lover was radiant. Her smile showed no sign of remorse. She kissed me tenderly and wrapped her arm around my neck.

"I'd like to be with you again," I said, in an intimate tone.

She pretended to be surprised.

"Why?"

I took the question as her way of discovering how I felt.

"Because you make love without holding back."

"Oh? Do you find me uptight?"

"Well, when you drink tea . . . yes."

Elizabeth laughed quietly.

"Let's just say that I didn't have a liberal upbringing."

We stayed in the bathroom for a few more minutes. I lowered my eyes so that she wouldn't see my victorious expression. This was a conquest, a triumph. I felt less poor, less alone. I also knew that this feeling would fade one day. So I promised myself that I'd get to know my lover, that I wouldn't see her as Mount Everest conquered, but as a woman with a heart and feelings. This promise would be difficult to keep. I didn't know if Elizabeth was willing to see me again. I had to hope that she was. Of course, I was impressed by her wealth. I'd surely give in to the desire to enjoy it in one way or another. Elizabeth wasn't fooled. She interpreted my silence for what it really was.

"You're just a child."

I frowned, more surprised than offended.

"But I want to make you happy," she added.

"I don't want to be kept."

"What exactly do you want to do with your life?"

"You asked me that question before. And I remember telling you that I had no idea."

"Yes, but . . . You have to earn a living. You can't rely on your family forever," she said, nodding in the direction of Bob and Koffi.

"I don't want to work in a factory like a lot of immigrants."

"Who told you about the factories?" she asked, wide-eyed.

"My friend, Eddy. He told me in his letters that if you don't have experience in Canada, you're doomed to work in a factory."

"Or you could go to school," she suggested, in a hushed voice.

"I'd need to know what I want to do."

"I could see you as a doctor. I think you're gifted."

She smiled again, and I kissed her on the lips.

"I really like you," she said. "That's clear."

We returned to the living room to join the other cheerful characters without another word. I let her precede me by a few minutes. The room was divided between dancers and spectators. The architect had let his wife dance with a younger man. He was watching them slyly. Elizabeth was at his side. Ann was chatting with Koffi between songs. Bob had gone back to his discussion, but the people to whom he was talking seemed more interested in the dancers. Maria walked by me, gave me a wink, which I ignored, and went straight to the bathroom. While she was gone, I helped myself to something to eat.

The architect pulled his cheque book out of his dark jacket. He jotted something down with his gold pen, then asked Elizabeth to give his wife the cheque. When the young woman looked at it, she laughed and blew her husband kisses. Maria returned and took me by the arm to dance. I knew that she understood what had happened. Koffi put on a Latin American rumba.

"So?" she whispered in my ear.

"So, what?"

"Don't try to stall. This is a long piece, so you don't stand a chance."

"I don't know what you're talking about."

"Listen, Ray, I might be tipsy, but I'm not stupid. You banged missus rich, didn't you?"

"There's no need to say it like that."

"Oh! Now we have to watch how we talk about Elizabeth."

I noticed that Elizabeth was looking at us.

"Why did you want to get into the bathroom?"

"To join you."

I stiffened instinctively.

"I'm teasing you . . . When you're drinking, you really need to go to the bathroom. I didn't know you two were in there. When I came back to sit down, I realized it was you. I don't care what you do with Elizabeth. All I ask is that you stop your stupid moralizing! From now on, we're in the same boat. Okay?"

"Ann's not my friend."

"She will be. Anyway, she and Koffi seem to be getting along very well."

The song ended. I quickly moved away so I wouldn't have to endure any more questions.

Elizabeth and I danced to a couple of songs as if we were strangers. She didn't make any comment about Maria.

The Sun Rises

Much later on, when the sun was rising and there were only a few guests left, Maria came over to me.

"Are you angry with me?"

"No. If it wasn't for you, I'd still be in the apartment thinking about my ghosts."

"What ghosts?"

"Oh, it's a long story. And I'm sure you're not interested."

"Yes, I am interested."

I sat down in a corner and started to tell her.

"I knew a girl named Catherine Maïmouna Dossou. Everyone called her the Bountiful Bijou . . ."

We eventually left the apartment. Elizabeth had retired to her room long before. In the car, Bob and Koffi fell asleep in the back seat. I continued my story. Maria drove slowly for once.

"If I drive fast, you won't have time to tell me everything!"

"I'll have time to tell you, if you stay friends with me."

She smiled, keeping her eyes on the road. The red car disappeared into the city, which was coming to life.

Last Words for a Parrot

Here are my final words for you, Cloclo. Do you remember when some poachers came, tore you away from your mother, and snatched you from your branch? Do you remember that first act of violence? The one that jeopardized your future among other parrots? I remember. I remember your heartrending cries at night, your pain at being plucked from the comforting smells and verdant colours of your natural habitat. And that sorrow is all the more familiar to me because I also experienced a departure with no return, an ablation from my ancestral homeland. The darkness of the first nights far away from a familiar place is a never-ending requiem. Of course, unlike you, I left of my own free will. But is fleeing misery really a choice? The will to leave in no way eases the loneliness in a foreign land. The redness of other people's sun has something blood-soaked about it the first time you set eyes on it. And the stars that you discover don't have the milkiness of those that nurtured your childhood.

Since we've both departed—you from a forest that scatters pearly light and me from a poor country that sometimes resonates in my bones at night—I must let you know something. I must tell you where you came from. You were born in an almost virgin area, in a hot, humid jungle. The blades of the leaves on the trees there are swollen with rainwater. One sunny day, a man tore you away from your forest. He abducted you. I wasn't the wildlife trader. I wasn't any kind of trader. That crook saw you only as an animal to be sold. Maybe that's how he still sees you. Even if, today, you can fly very high and you speak wonderfully. For you see, you have to be loved not to fear being sold.

Before you fly off again to other places, before ancient trees carry you to freedom, I have to tell you that I've found happiness. I'm happy to love a city that's too large for me to penetrate all its secrets. Toronto is my jungle, and the faces of its inhabitants hide the secret of its life like the water-swollen blades of the leaves in your forest. I no longer feel wounded when I think about Bijou and all those who taught me to love. The embers of my wounds are slowly cooling under the layers of snow in this country. The cold soothes the pain as long as the memories remain warm.

Today, many people ask me where I come from. I tell them I was born in Toronto. I'm talking about my second birth because you never remember the first. The second one always happens in a stupefying din, in a world that's collapsing. Every moment, a new soul is born for the second time. I imagine those selves being lost, forlorn, holding onto ghosts in their memories. Then little by little, like me, they learn to walk again like a child who's come into the world. They rediscover words, meanings, and all of humanity. Like me, they come back to life.

At this hour, there's not so much as a cat moving outside. Or should I say a parrot? I would've dearly loved to fly like you, Cloclo! Unfortunately, we're only born twice.

Translator's Acknowledgements

Many are the people who contributed to the English version of this novel. My thanks to Lee Heppner for her careful revision of the translation, Debby Dubrofsky for her astute reading of the English text, Pénélope Mallard for her insight into some of the French expressions, and everyone at Mawenzi House for their steadfast support and professionalism. My sincere gratitude to the author, Didier Leclair, for his unwavering assistance throughout this project.